D1558828

ENDZ CASINO

&

RESORT

A NOVELLA BY

BEN LARRACEY

for Stacy

1

Wes DeLeo woke to ringing slot machines and coins falling. An attack on all his senses. The constant barrage of a casino in full motion. Its peak hour.

In a daze, DeLeo lifted his head from the green felt poker table and opened his eyes. The casino was empty. The tables and slot machines abandoned. Any sign of people was gone. He squinted and scratched his head. Was I dreaming, he thought?

Confusion struck him. Half drank glasses of wine and beer bottles were left on tables and next to silently flashing slot machines. Next to him a cigarette butt smoldered in an ashtray. DeLeo was alone.

He reached for one of the poker chips in front of him and spun it between his fingers. His vision blurry, it took a moment to focus. In gold type font across the chip, it read: Endz Casino & Resort.

Endz Casino? Where am I? He thought, and how did I get here?

He tried to replay the night before. Maybe it was still night. It was impossible to tell what time it was in here. No clocks, no people to ask.

The last thing he remembered was a dive bar—a solo acoustic show, somewhere outside of Cleveland. He recalled that for sure. However, a casino? He didn't remember a casino. He didn't even know of a casino around here—if he was still in Cleveland—especially one this nice. Impossible. This felt like Las Vegas.

He rubbed his eyes and saw color spots. He remembered lights. Blue neon car headlights burned into the back of his mind.

Did he drink too much and blackout? He did that from time to time. Part of the life of being a touring musician. He didn't feel drunk or hungover. His mind was clear but foggy, like abruptly waking up from a deep sleep.

Maybe I was drugged, he thought.

He reached in the pocket of his gray cardigan for his phone. Empty except for a few pieces of fuzz and lint. He checked his black jeans for the keys to his old van— nothing. No phone, no wallet. He looked to his left then right for his guitar. An acoustic Gibson with burnt yellow coloring and black finish. The most expensive thing he ever bought and many would argue the most important thing in his life. He would never leave that behind no matter how drunk he got. Never.

Cold sweat seeped from his pores at the thought of his guitar stolen. He could never replace it, especially not now. He had bought it during a time in his life when he had a few extra bucks and his music was selling.

"Welcome to Endz Casino and Resort," a smoky voice said from a large TV monitor folding down from the ceiling.

Startled by the abrupt noise cutting through the silence, DeLeo saw the same golden yellow font of "Endz" spin into the frame. The graphics clicked and jumped like footage from some old commercial.

"The finest resort town around." The narrator's voice continued in an old fashioned, hollow, five pack a day cigarette sound, like some long dead Hollywood icon that no one remembered anymore.

Desaturated footage of lush green lawns with pink flamingos scattered about followed the Endz tittle card.

"It's easy to find but nearly impossible to leave," the voice continued. "We have the best: gambling, service, relaxation, nightlife."

The barrage of footage that followed showed images of crowded casino floors, happy guests winning lots of money. A packed ballroom of drunken revilers danced under a crystal chandelier. Overweight men and woman lounged poolside drinking the happy hour special. A middle-aged man chomped on an oversized cigar, while a masseur's hands disappeared into his back fat. Nearby, a woman smoked a Virginia Slim and received a pedicure to her yellowing toenails.

"And don't forget the world famous buffet," the fat man said into the camera rolling his wet cigar to the corner of his mouth.

The footage changed to the same fat man standing in front of a massive buffet, his belly tight and ready to pop like a boiled sausage. He scooped cheesy eggs and spoonfuls of bacon onto his plate.

The advertisement abruptly ended, and the screen went black. The casino returned to the quiet of the ventilation system pumping recycled air in from above.

"Sir, would you like to play?" A voice startled DeLeo. It was the same smoky, almost British sounding voice of the narrator on the commercial, but this time in person.

A Dealer now stood at the poker table. He wore a white shirt, black bow-tie, vest with bands around his sleeves.

How he got there, and so quickly, DeLeo had no idea, but he felt relieved he could finally get some questions answered.

"I'm sorry," DeLeo said, trying to be polite. "I didn't see you there before." He rubbed his eyes. The blank, distant stare of the Dealer looking back at him made him uncomfortable. The guy didn't seem to blink.

DeLeo nervously laughed, "I must have had a rough night or something. Could you tell me where I am?"

The Dealer pulled out a deck of cards and shuffled. "You're at the Endz Resort and Casino sir."

DeLeo pointed at the TV which just played the commercial and tried to be polite. "I know. You see, I can't find my phone."

"—Oh, you won't need that here sir." The Dealer said interrupting DeLeo. The Dealer shuffled his deck of cards and began to deal.

Annoyed, DeLeo gently put his hand on the Dealer's arm, stopping him from laying the cards on the table and said, "Can you stop doing that please?"

The Dealer instantly returned to his cold, distant stare.

"Sorry," DeLeo said, unable to tell if the Dealer was annoyed at him touching his arm. "Please, I'm a little out of it. How did I get here?"

The Dealer raised his hand pointing to the slowly revolving door at the entrance to the casino. "You came in through the door."

DeLeo was losing his patience. "Where is everyone?" he asked now more directly. "I heard voices. There were people here."

"We have our good and bad days," the Dealer replied with an indifference that infuriated DeLeo.

"You're a hard guy to read huh?" DeLeo clenched his jaw.

"Are you ready to play now sir?"

"Play what?" DeLeo stepped away from the poker table.

"I don't even know where the hell I am, and you've been playing games with me the whole time."

"Very well sir," the Dealer responded indifferently.

For the next ten minutes, DeLeo wandered the casino floor, passing still smoldering cigarettes, poker chips left on tables, coins in slot machines. The Dealer seemed to follow DeLeo's every move as he walked through the casino. His melon shaped head swiveled unnaturally. His eyes like an owl, cold and non-blinking, observed DeLeo's every step from a distance.

"Can I help you?" DeLeo yelled from across the casino.

"Are you ready to play yet, sir?" The Dealers voice hollow and without emotion.

DeLeo ignored the Dealer and headed toward the double doors at the end of the casino aisle. He opened the doors only to find bricks. A wall of brown and red bricks stacked floor to ceiling.

Huh?

DeLeo opened the next set of double doors a few aisles away — more bricks.

"Is this place under construction or something?" DeLeo yelled across the casino floor. A blank stare answered his question.

"What's going on here? What type of place is this?" DeLeo snapped walking back toward the poker table.

"Are you ready to play now sir?" The Dealer asked.

"I'm not going to play a game with you," DeLeo pointed to the revolving door. "I take it that's the only way out of here, huh?"

"I wouldn't go out there," the Dealer advised.

"Why not?"

"It's not safe sir. I can't protect you out there."

"Protect me from what?"

"Protect you from what's out there. Please sit."

"Really?" DeLeo asked rhetorically, then walked out of the casino through the revolving door.

2

A cold, still darkness, and faint smell of sulfur greeted DeLeo when he exited the casino. His eyes adjusted to the now almost complete darkness. In front of him lay a massive city, or the remains of one. Enormous high-rises without a single light stretched into the night above. The skyline was like the top of a busted picket fence or a row of chipped and rotted teeth.

Abandoned cars scattered the street in front of DeLeo and slowly disappeared into the pale encroaching fog snaking through the old stone buildings. Not even the remote glow of a headlight or phone couldn't be seen anywhere.

Endz Casino & Resort was at the base of a massive dark tower that stretched into the coal-colored sky above. The only source of light came from the flashing casino sign droning on behind DeLeo.

"Hello?" DeLeo yelled into the darkness. His voice echoing back.

No one was here. Not a soul. The city seemed completely empty. Creepy. A chill ran up DeLeo's spine. He was tempted to go back inside, but a shiny brass railing in front of him caught his attention. He thought it strange and out of place. It was something out of an awards show or special event.

The railing stretched past the abandoned cars and disappeared like everything else. Underneath the brass railing was a blood red carpet that ran along the damp asphalt.

"Hello?" DeLeo said again. His voice cracked this time. It was the silence that unnerved DeLeo more than the darkness. His curiosity got the best of him, and he moved down the carpet.

Where is everyone? He thought.

He froze at the sound of movement. It was close, but how close he couldn't tell. The noise wasn't quite a footstep, but it was something. Suddenly a rat scurried across the carpet and vanished into the darkness. DeLeo jumped at the sight of the rat.

He calmed himself and continued.

The fog seemed to be getting thicker the further away he got from the casino. He looked back. The casino was further away than he thought. A hundred, maybe a hundred and fifty feet.

His ears perked at the sound of something in the shadows. It was different this time. He tried to place it. It wasn't a footstep, but a dragging sound. Maybe a scraping sound against the wet asphalt.

It was time to go back he thought. There was nothing out here. Just talk to the Dealer, and play his game. Do whatever he wants and get the hell out of here.

DeLeo started to head back, but the casino was gone. The fog was too thick. Cold sweat ran down his back. He had gone too far. He started to panic and squinted into the darkness. He remembered the red carpet and looked down. Nothing. Only the cold wet asphalt was beneath his feet.

You idiot, DeLeo wailed in his mind. What were you thinking?

"Hello?" he whispered into the fog, alarmed now. "Is anyone there?"

The slow dragging sound returned. The outline of something moved in the fog. It looked like a person, but he couldn't be sure. It stood on two legs but hunched over. The arms were too long. Its posture crooked. Its head abnormally large. The figure stood in the cover of the fog, its giant arms slowly swinging back and forth like the pendulums of an old grandfather clock.

DeLeo didn't move a muscle. His heart beat faster. What was it doing? Did it see him? Hear him?

The slow groveling sound continued. There were more of them, whatever they were. A groan came from the dark followed by another one.

"If you come near me I'll mess you up!' DeLeo yelled. He waited for whatever response was imminent, but there was nothing.

Suddenly he felt a tug on his pant leg. He almost shrieked in freight. A soft voice whispered, "Shh."

"Huh?" DeLeo responded. Sheer horror was plastered across his face at the thought of what those things were. He looked down. A woman, maybe thirty, delicate and grimy looking put her skinny finger to her chapped lips.

"SHH," she repeated then pointed to the figure back-lit by the mist, its long arms slowly swaying back and forth.

"What is it?" DeLeo asked in barely a whispered.

"Quiet," the woman mouthed without making a sound. She gently put her hand on DeLeo's mouth to get him to stop talking and said, "They're fast." She clasped DeLeo's sweaty hand. "Get ready to run."

DeLeo's heart sank into a slow deep thud at the implication of her words. The muscle thundered in his chest cavity, shaking him with every pump.

DeLeo felt the woman squeeze his hand tighter and slowly nod. Whatever it was, it was going to happen soon.

Suddenly he felt her tug, and before he knew it, he was running as fast as he could.

His lungs burned as he followed the woman blindly through the night. All he could see was what was right in front of him. Abandoned cars, damaged street lights dangling above.

A crash came from behind them, followed by a groan. Whatever those things were, they were chasing them.

"Fast!" The woman yelled, this time not bothering to whisper.

DeLeo followed the woman's every step and turn. His eyes watered from the cold air, but it didn't matter. She was his eyes. His only job was to run and not trip over anything. DeLeo could hear the grunting and groaning of those things not far behind them now. From the sound, he tried to determine how many there were. There had to be more than three or four, but it was tough tell. The sounds blended together.

After running for what seemed like a block or two a structure emerged from the dark, an old building made of brick and stone.   "In here," the woman yelled pulling him toward the building.

A cloud of dust coughed up when they entered. They wcrc in a lobby of some kind. Chairs were flipped over and scattered all over the bleak room. DeLeo knew it was an old bank at the sight of the teller stations.

"This way," the woman said pointing to the back.

A loud crash of shattering glass exploded from behind them. DeLeo looked back and saw six of those grotesque things jump through the bank window. He couldn't make out their features. He could only hear their snarl. All he knew for sure was they weren't human.

In the back of the bank there was a large, closed vault made of solid steel. The woman picked up a wrench lying next to the door and started banging. She screamed in a blind panic, frightening DeLeo even more.

The creatures were getting closer. The violent hammering on the door echoed through the small bank corridor and certainly gave away their location.

DeLeo peered around the corner. He still couldn't make them out, but they glistened in the darkness. They seemed slimy, like the skin of a frog or snake. Some creature. One looked up at DeLeo with giant black pupils. From his brief glimpse in the dark, it looked like nothing he had ever seen or knew existed.

"Hurry!" DeLeo shouted. Sweat poured from his face at the sight of the beasts coming down the corridor.

The woman banged on the vault door even harder. DeLeo's ears rang.

"Open up!" She screamed. "I'm back! Open!"

Suddenly, latches and bolt locks clicked from the inside of the vault and the door opened. They quickly entered.

The vault door slammed behind them, the steel on steel mechanism locking it securely. The concrete floor shook beneath DeLeo. A short silence followed, then the scratching and clawing of fingernails against steel came from outside.

DeLeo backed away from the entrance praying the old steel vault would hold. The scratching turned violent and chaotic before changing into a frenzy of banging, then suddenly there was nothing.

Silence.

"What the hell were those things?" DeLeo looked for the woman in the darkness of the vault.

He saw her run to a nearby table, grab an object and flip it over. In the dim flicker of lantern light DeLeo realized it was an hourglass. The white sand slowly falling through the tiny opening, sparkling like water across a pond.

"What is that?" DeLeo asked.

"That was too close," DeLeo heard a booming voice say. A male voice from somewhere in the vault.

They weren't alone.

DeLeo let his eyes adjust to the golden glow of the small lantern illuminating the room. He saw three faces, all wide-eyed staring back at him. Light beamed across the parts of their faces that didn't fall in shadow. A woman, forties, with red hair wearing a large cloth dress, like the Mennonites or Amish. In her arms, a teenager sat curled on the floor. He was maybe fourteen, had messy hair and wore a Nirvana t-shirt. The third wide-eyed face staring at De-Leo belonged to a clean-cut, young man wearing a varsity jacket. He was college-aged and looked terrified.

DeLeo knew the deep male voice couldn't have come from any of them. He was about to speak when the booming baritone cut through the silence again.

"Where have you been? I've, we've," the voice corrected himself, " been worried sick about you Sadie."

DeLeo looked in the direction of the voice. A large police officer with a square, serious face stepped out of the dark and into the glare of the lantern. He was both tall and wide, not fat, but muscular. He wore a blue uniform and the large leather boots of a state trooper. A leather harness across his barrel chest connected to his firearm on his hip.

DeLeo strained his eyes in the dark looking for the woman, Sadie—the cop had called her. Maybe she could give him some information, he thought.

Sadie walked into the glow of the light. Her eyes were hollow and distant. DeLeo could tell she was afraid of the massive police officer. She kept her distance from him and avoided all eye contact, making sure to keep the small table with the lantern between them.

The officer rounded the table and moved closer to DeLeo "Who is this guy?" the officer asked Sadie.

"I found him out there, alone," Sadie said timidly. Her eyes darted anywhere but toward the officer.

"What's going on?" DeLeo interrupted, "What the hell were those things back there?"

The officer ignored DeLeo and addressed everyone in the vault but him. "We have to protect ourselves. We can't take in strangers whenever we want. We don't have enough food or supplies."

"There's plenty of food John," Sadie said. DeLeo could tell she was nervous. Sadie grabbed the lantern off the table and walked to the back of the room. Hundreds of canned foods; vegetables, pasta, fruit, lined the wooden shelving. "Just because you're a cop doesn't mean you get to run the show," Sadie yelled. Her eyes turned to DeLeo, who was beginning to feel like he was now in a place with a whole new set of problems.

"He was out there alone, with nothing," Sadie added, "and those things would have gotten him if I left him."

DeLeo watched the cop, John, and waited for an explosive reaction. He was caught off guard when John's demeanor changed to soft and caring, almost fatherly tone. "I was just worried about you Sadie. We can't afford to lose you too." John walked over to Sadie, rubbed her back and adjusted her hair.

Sadie looked at the ground embarrassed, uncomfortable.

What did I walk into, DeLeo thought to himself. Questions shot through his mind: who are these people? How long have they been here and what the hell was going on?

DeLeo observed the blank faces in the vault and their reaction to the way John was acting toward Sadie. The twenty-something in the varsity jacket looked away pretending not to notice, scraping mud off the soles of his Doc Martins. The woman in the oversized religious dress was different. She stared right at Sadie, scowling like it was her she hated. Like Sadie was the problem, not John. The woman continued to hold the teenage boy in the Nirvana t-shirt in her arms, comforting him like a small puppy or baby.

The teenager seemed not to care, indifferent to the whole thing. His eyes glossed over in what appeared to be fear. DeLeo couldn't know for sure. Was it from those things outside, John, or the crazy lady that seemed to hold him over-protectively like his doll? Then the woman spoke, never taking her eyes off Sadie.

"Everything is going to be okay Billy," the woman said, adjusting the excess dress fabric under her while rubbing the boy's head. "Everything is going to be okay. I'm going to keep you safe. There's nothing to worry about."

The college kid looked up from his shoes and spoke with reservation. "John, give her some space huh?" His voice cracked as he spoke, like the final stages of puberty. "She's had a rough time out there and so what if we add another to the group?"

"What was that Tucker? Know-it-all college boy?" John snapped. His piercing eyes reflected the dull lantern light.

DeLeo could tell Tucker was scared to death of John by the way he was overcome with nervous laughter. "I just meant she must be tired and might need some rest. That's all," Tucker stuttered.

Tucker stood up and grabbed two bottles of water from the shelf, walked over to Sadie and DeLeo and handed them the water. "It's from my share," Tucker said to, John eyeing the transaction.

"It better be," John said.

"My name is Tucker smiled at DeLeo. "That's Billy," Tucker said pointing to the teen in the Nirvana shirt. "Ethel is next to him," Tucker said pointing at the scowling red-headed woman. "You already know Sadie, and the big guy right here is John."

DeLeo finally got a good look at John, who now stood

in the light. He was easily a foot taller than him, his mouth pencil thin and hard.

"I'm going to pat you down okay?" John said, moving closer.

"Is he serious?" DeLeo asked Tucker.

"Eyes here," John snapped. Spit from his lips hit DeLeo in the face.

"Just do whatever he says," Sadie said, her voice defeated and weak.

DeLeo let John search him. The room returned to quiet as John found nothing. Moments later DeLeo was walking around the room waiting for someone to speak first. The vault was twenty by twenty. In the back there was floor to ceiling shelving that DeLeo imagined once held money; now it seem to have endless amounts of expired canned food. Beans, olives, corn, spaghetti-o's. Next to the shelf was a curtain. DeLeo looked behind it. A piss-smelling, five-gallon white pail sat in the corner. Dark yellow dehydrated piss floated at the bottom.

DeLeo shut the curtain and addressed the room, "Is anyone going to tell me what those things are out there?" He looked from face to face. Everyone avoided his eye contact. Finally, DeLeo turned to Tucker and grabbed his varsity jacket.

"Tell me?!"

Tucker let out a long breath, "We honestly know as much as you."

DeLeo didn't believe him. "Endz Casino," DeLeo shouted, "never heard of it. I seriously doubt I know as much as you."

DeLeo watched Tucker glance at the others in the room. Obviously, they had discussed their situation and how they each had gotten there before.

"We all have our theories," Tucker said.

"What do you think?" DeLeo said.

Tucker hesitated, then spoke, "I think it's the government. You know some experiment, like how the CIA experimented on people using LSD back in the fifties. I think this is the same thing."

"Shut up," John's voice blared from the corner of the steel room. "It's not the government you idiot, or aliens, or any of that hippie shit. So if I hear one more word about conspiracy theories, I'm going to throw you out there with those fuckers. Got me?"

Tucker shrugged. He wasn't going to argue with John. "That's just my opinion," he said, in a tone implying it didn't matter.

"I believe you," Billy said, looking up from Ethel's arms.

"Thanks." Tucker forced a smile.

In the faint glimmer of the lamp light, DeLeo saw Ethel squeeze Billy tighter. She whispered in his ear, "Don't listen to him, Billy. John is the one who will protect us." Ethel lifted her head, her eyes the color of ice. She scanned the room until she locked eyes with DeLeo.

"It's much worse than the government," she said with absolute conviction. "I knew this would happen. It was only a matter of time. We are being judged. It's time you get right with God or suffer the fate of those things outside."

"Enough with that crazy talk," Sadie said from the corner. "God has nothing to do with this."

"Slut," Ethel said under her breath. "You wish the Lord had nothing to do with this because you live a life of sin."

"Ethel, why don't you let go of Billy," Tucker said coming to Sadie's defense. "Give him some space. You're not even his mother."

"Blasphemy! How dare you. I know you have feelings for this little hussy, but never question me again."

"Enough of this shit!" John shouted. 'Everyone just shut

the fuck up. All that matters is staying alive. That's it. Nothing else."

DeLeo watched the fragile people in front of him begin to fracture, and the thought of the Dealer and his eerie stare came to mind.

"There was a man back there, wasn't there?" DeLeo asked, curious and wishing to stop the situation from deteriorating even further. "Who was he?" It seemed to work. Everyone's attention was now drawn back to him.

"A man?" Sadie asked. A puzzled look in her eye, "I didn't see anyone with you."

"The Dealer, at the casino," DeLeo implored. "He said something about playing a game."

"Look, pal," John said standing up and walking toward him. The hard soles of his knee-high leather boots thumping against the concrete floor. The buckle of his holster rubbed against the nylon of his belt. "I don't know what you're trying to do here, sow a little dissent or plant a seed of false hope, but no one here has heard or seen any dealer. Or been to any casino, so you best either shut up or tell us something."

"I swear, I'm telling you the truth." DeLeo looked to Sadie for support. "It was right where you found me. Through the fog somewhere. It couldn't have been more than two hundred feet away."

John asked Sadie, "You see anything?"

Sadie avoided eye contact and looked to the ground shaking her head, "No. I didn't see anything."

"Sadie," DeLeo said. "I'm not lying."

"I'm sorry, I just didn't see it."

DeLeo knew what he saw. The Dealer, the casino, all of that was real. And god forbid if he was going to spend another second in the same vault with these nuts. This steel tomb was just a match away from exploding. The casino couldn't be far he thought. Maybe the fog had cleared. 'I'm not lying," DeLeo walked toward the door. "I'll show you."

John's massive frame blocked the vault door, surprising DeLeo by how fast he moved.

"You touch that door pal, and I'll break your arm," John growled.

DeLeo stopped and tried to explain himself, but no words came to his mouth, "I'm just –"

"John he's scaring Billy," Ethel said from the back of the vault. She squeezed Billy.

"I'm just –" DeLeo tried again to justify his case but quickly regretted it as John's large hand grabbed his chest.

"You touch that door, and I'll break your neck." John pulled DeLeo closer. He could feel the heat radiating off John like a furnace.

"I'm in charge," John said in a gravelly whisper. "Now," John let out a steamy breath, "Sit down!" he roared pushing, DeLeo so hard he fell to the ground.

Sadie rushed to DeLeo's side, "Are you okay?" She turned to John "Why did you do that?"

John ignored her and returned to one of the dark corners of the vault.

"I'm fine," DeLeo said standing up and brushing off the bits of dust and dirt. "I'm fine." He scanned the room. No one seemed to care what just happened. They were all prisoners here, not only to the beast outside, but to John in here.

"John's a good man," Ethel said to DeLeo. "He's just trying to keep the peace."

"Is that so?" DeLeo asked rhetorically, knowing whose side she was on.

"Let's pray," Ethel said reaching out her hand, "the Lord Almighty only lets those who love him into his house."

DeLeo had caused enough problems and reluctantly gave Ethel his hand. Billy reached next to him and grabbed Tucker's hand. John joined from his chair.

DeLeo noticed bandages on both of Billy's wrists. He had seen that type of injury a long time ago with one of his high school friends.

"Oh, he's fine," Ethel said quickly to DeLeo, in a fine southern accent, almost as if she knew what he was thinking. "Now let us pray."

DeLeo bowed his head with everyone else. When Ethel was a good way into her prayer, DeLeo lifted his head, watching the others. It was all nonsense to him.

Sadie gazed at DeLeo and smiled. She wasn't praying either. He liked her. She seemed like the only normal one offering any ray of hope. Sadie then rolled her eyes and made her hand in the shape of a gun and pretended to shoot herself in the head.

DeLeo chuckled.

Ethel and the others continued to pray, oblivious to Sadie's mockery. DeLeo bit his bottom lip. Sadie winked, continuing to try and make him laugh. DeLeo smirked, rolled his eyes, and pretended to tie a noose around his neck, all the while, unbeknownst to them, John was watching,with more than a hint of jealousy.

4

"Nice shirt," DeLeo said referring to Billy's Nirvana shirt, trying to make conversation.

"Thanks," Billy rubbed the creases out. "You a fan?"

"I am. I was always more of a Soundgarden fan, but I like all the Seattle stuff: Alice in Chains, Pearl Jam. Anything by Chris Cornell really."

"You a musician?" Sadie asked, enthused. "I mean you look like one," she added.

"Really? I didn't know I was that obvious. I play guitar and sing."

"Wow," Sadie said blushing. Her eyelashes flickered like butterfly wings.

"Musicians," John mocked from the corner. "Bunch of freeloaders. You're a little old to be chasing a kid's dream, aren't you? What are you? Thirty-five, forty? Your pathetic attempt to chase tail? What's your real job? Welfare fraud?" John laughed at his own words.

DeLeo ignored him. The truth was he had found some minor success in his twenties. A song on a TV show he never watched, sometimes a royalty check came. It had been tough making money since then.

"Do you have any groupies?" Sadie asked, raising an eyebrow.

DeLeo blushed. He couldn't believe she was asking these questions in front of everyone. In any other circumstance it would have been fine, but here she was coming on strong.

"I miss music," Sadie lamented. "You know they used to call me Sexy Sadie, like the Beatles song. You like the Beatles?"

"Of course," DeLeo said, happy to change the subject back to music.

Sadie twirled her hair. "I miss beautiful things," she gazed DeLeo directly in her eyes. "Do you think I'm beautiful?"

DeLeo felt uncomfortable. Their conversation was getting a bit awkward for this place, especially in front of these people.

"You know I used to play piano," Tucker said trying to gain Sadie's affection.

"Nobody cares Tucker," John bellowed from the corner, his eyes locked on Sadie.

"So, are you married? You have a girlfriend?" Sadie said inching toward DeLeo.

DeLeo froze. He felt uncomfortable. It seemed like everyone in the room was watching his interaction with Sadie.

"Um…," DeLeo searched for a way to change the subject. "So.....does anyone remember how they got here? All I remember was I was at a club finishing an acoustic set, and then suddenly there were bright lights. Like headlights or something. Then I woke up at the..." he stopped before he said casino, "then I woke up here."

"The same for me," Sadie added. "One minute I was at

work and then the next I was here. It's all still so foggy."

Ethel laughed. "At work, you say? A strip club isn't work."

"I'm a dancer," Sadie shot back.

"You're a whore. A creature of the night. You fit in well here," Ethel smiled to herself, satisfied with her insult.

Sadie pulled back her hair, "Aren't you the martyr, all high and mighty and dressed like a pilgrim."

"God has left you alone sister. I'll pray extra hard for you."

DeLeo watched the back and forth continue between the two women until it was interrupted by John screeching his chair across the concrete floor.

"This is a waste of time," John said. "It doesn't matter. I'm a cop. Sadie's a…a dancer — so what?" John turned his frustration toward DeLeo. "Are we supposed to team up like a group of super heroes? The Avengers? Each of us with some fucking special power, and you're our leader right?" John continued toward DeLeo. "Not on my watch."

"That's not what I meant," DeLeo attempted to defend himself against the brute of a man standing in front of him. "I just want to know why the hell we're here!"

"Remember, everything was fine until you got here." John pointed at the hourglass. Sand still fell. "Consider this a job interview. A trial period. Your time to prove yourself before time runs out. Now let's get some shuteye," John returned to his dark corner. "We need to be rested up. We'll only have an hour maybe two once those things are gone."

Everyone prepared for bed. Ethel and Billy moved to one of the empty corners, Tucker to another.

Sadie tossed DeLeo a blanket. "It's not much, but it's something."

"Thanks," DeLeo said and wrapped the blanket around himself. The fabric was coarse like sandpaper. "I don't know what's more dangerous those things out there or him," DeLeo whispered to Sadie, motioning to John, who sat stoically on the other side of the vault cleaning his gun.

"He's just trying to scare you," Sadie said, trying to comfort him.

"Well, it's working."

John snapped his gun shut. The click of metal on metal caused chills to run up DeLeo's spine. "Getting a little close over there aren't we?" John hissed from the corner.

"Just giving him a little advice," Sadie said, winking at DeLeo.

"A little close for advice in my opinion," John said lying down on the ground. He pulled up a blanket and rested his revolver on his belly. The silver barrel glinting in the light.

DeLeo sat on the ground, preparing to lie down.

Sadie crouched down in front of him. "You know," Sadie whispered, "if you want you can come to my corner."

"Here? Now?" DeLeo said, startled she would even ask him, "I don't know." He nodded to the corners where John and Ethel lay.

"I don't belong to him," Sadie said, taking offense.

"That's not what I meant," DeLeo reassured her, sensing that she had gotten the wrong impression.

"Well," she smiled. "If you get lonely, I'm right over there.

DeLeo swallowed and watched her disappear into the dark vault. He knew John must have been watching them. He always seemed to be keeping an eye on her.

An hour must have passed but DeLeo couldn't tell. Time had no meaning here. He just watched the flame dance around the lantern. The deep snore of John sleeping put DeLeo at ease. At least the beast was asleep, he thought to himself.

Just as DeLeo shut his eyes and started to relax, he felt a

hand on his leg and then the warm breath of someone next to him. It was Sadie. The curls of her hair brushing his face and her sweet scent gave her away. She exhaled on his neck and whispered, "shhhhhh."

DeLeo froze. He didn't know what to do. She kissed his lips. He felt her tongue against his mouth and her arms wrapping around him.

DeLeo quickly pulled her away. "I can't," he whispered, barely audible. "Not here. Not now. Please don't."

Sadie scowled. Her face barely visible in the dark. Then he felt Sadie slowly inch away from him, and a great sense of relief washed over him.

He had to get out of here, away from these people. As soon as the hourglass cleared and John opened the vault door, he was gone. No second thoughts. Gone. He had to get back to the Dealer.

DeLeo turned away from Sadie and closed his eyes. He needed to at least try and get some rest. He shut his eyes and drifted off to sleep. Flashes of a dingy rock club entered his mind. Dark lighting, a bar lined with brown liquor. Naked pin-up girls with retro hairstyles littered the wall next to old newspapers with music headlines from eras long gone.

The spotlight blinded DeLeo as he sat on stage singing his heart out, only his acoustic guitar separating him from the night owls high on whatever concoction of drugs and alcohol they were able to manage.

DeLeo finished the song, and someone from the crowd passed him a shot. He drank it. Suddenly more lights, head-lights—screeching rubber on the pavement. A car horn.

DeLeo suddenly woke up to the sound of screaming. He was disoriented, everything was blurry.

"Help!" A woman shrieked. It was Sadie.

DeLeo looked over to her corner. There was movement,

but it was too dark. He couldn't see anything.

"Get it off!" Sadie screamed again.

DeLeo's heart raced as a figured blurred by him. A gigantic shape. Did one of those creatures get inside? He couldn't tell. Whatever it was, it was big, strong, and fast.

The sound of thuds and flesh hitting flesh came from the dark corner. Sadie's corner. A loud squeal pierced the room. DeLeo couldn't tell who or what it was. All he could make out was the jagged and violent motioned of a figure pounding something.

Suddenly the room erupted in light. Ethel had turned up the lantern. The blaze blinded DeLeo. Thumps of flesh against flesh and screams filled his ears, but he still couldn't see anything.

A moment passed. DeLeo squinted his eyes. Ethel stood next to the lantern, a look of sheer horror on her face.

DeLeo followed Ethel's gaze toward Sadie's corner. John had Tucker by the neck pinned against the wall. Tucker's feet hung a foot off the ground. His face bloodied, lip swollen, face growing more and more purple from asphyxiation by the second.

Sadie ran toward DeLeo grabbing him by the shoulder, sobbing in his arms.

"Don't you ever touch her again," John roared at Tucker, an inch from his face.

"Please Wes, help me! I want to go. I want to leave," Sadic cried into DcLeo's shoulder. He stared helpless across the vault at John and Tucker. John let go of Tucker's neck and he fell to the ground, gasping for breath. Tucker curled up on the floor like a spider just before it dies.

John unholstered his sidearm, the lantern catching a glint of silver gunmetal, and cocked the pistol. He pointed it at DeLeo, no more than a foot away from his face.

"Did you touch her too?" John asked through a clenched

jaw.

DeLeo looked to Sadie for support, who still sobbed into his chest. He wanted help, he wanted answers, but every-one seemed to be falling into hysteria.

John walked forward, the pistol now an inch from his forehead. The angle of the shadow cut across John's square face and made him look like a madman. "I said, did you touch her?"

DeLeo started to shake his head but was too afraid. He adjusted his shoulder trying to get Sadie's attention hop-ing she would get this lunatic to settled down. DeLeo stut-tered, "Sad-di-die."

In one fluid motion, Sadie flung her head facing John. Her eyes smudged with mascara, fresh tears falling. "So what if he did," Sadie yelled, with everything ounce of passion she had in her, "I don't belong to you!"

DeLeo cringed. His blood ran cold.

"If I want to screw everyone in the room, I'll do it if I want. Stop trying to control me!" Sadie yelled.

DeLeo tried to step in quickly as possible, but couldn't get any words out. He was panicking and didn't know if it would only make things worse.

"And yes, I did fuck him," Sadie screamed violently at John, "right before you went to sleep. How do you like that? And you were to stupid to even notice."

DeLeo dropped his shoulders expecting a bullet through the top of his skull.

"If it wasn't for me," John said through his tight lips, "That thing over there," he pointed to Tucker with his gun, who still lay on the floor in a fetal position, "would have had his way with you. That right college boy?" John con-tinued motioning to Tucker, who was covered with tears and snot on the floor.

"I didn't do anything!" DeLeo finally sputtered, barely

getting the words out.

"Shut up!" John returned the gun to DeLeo's face.

Stupid decision, DeLeo thought. Keep your mouth shut.

"You look strung out," John turned the gun like a dagger twisting into a victim's spine. "Just like all the other musicians hopped up on something. What is it heroin? Coke?"

"What are we going to do with him?" Ethel blurted into the conversation. Her red hair roared like fire and her nose was held high. She motioned to Tucker, while gently stroking Billy's head.

John dropped the firearm from DeLeo's face and paced around the room. "I don't know, woman. Let me think. There has to law and order, without consequences there is only chaos." John stopped to catch his breath. Sweat poured down his face, his eyes glossy. "We banish him," John said, the thought seeming to come to him right at that very moment. "We put him outside. Lock the door. He could try again with Sadie or even with you Ethel. We never know."

"But those things, they're still out there," Billy pointed out, struggling a little bit from Ethel's embrace.

"They'll be gone soon enough, child," Ethel said, rubbing Billy's head and admiring John's command of the situation. "Soon enough."

DeLeo looked at the hourglass. It was almost empty; the last grains of sand were falling. Sadie nestled up to DeLeo, caressing his ncck. He pushed her away and she giggled hysterically, like some kind of mental patient.

John walked over to Tucker and kicked him in the gut. "What did you have to go and do that for, Tucker? Did you think there wouldn't be consequences? Now you're making me the bad guy. I hate being the bad guy." John kicked him again.

Tucker gasped for air.

"Stop it!" Billy yelled, trying to squeeze out of Ethel's overbearing, motherly grasp.

"Billy you're too young to understand," John said taking a condescending, paternal tone. "There need to be rules for a society to function. There must be laws, and Tucker broke one of those laws. He needs to be punished." John looked to Sadie, for her opinion. "What should be done?"

"Whatever you think. Banish him then," Sadie said indifferently, turning towards Wes again.

John grabbed Tucker by his college varsity coat and dragged him to his feet. "You can walk kid. I didn't kick you that hard."

"Wait!" Ethel screamed. The light from the lantern was like fire in her pupils. "Banishment? No, no, no – he needs to be punished. Even if the little whore did bring it on herself. He couldn't survive out there," Ethel pointed her bony finger at everyone in the room, "If we banish him...and then what? Two, three days he'll come crawling back to us looking for redemption? No, no, no. We can't just cast him out. We need to stamp out this evil before it spreads and consumes us from within." Ethel slammed her fist against the table, shaking the lantern.

John dragged Tucker to the vault door, and made him open it. He raised his pistol, preparing himself for whatever waited for them outside.

A rush of cold sulfur smelling air entered the small space. Outside it was black. A black so dark it seemed to absorb all the color in the vault. On the back of the vault door were large, inch deep claw marks leftover from whatever had chased them in.

"Please, don't make me go out there," Tucker begged, tears, blood, and drool flowing down his once cleanly shaved face. John shoved his pistol into Tucker's back and they left the vault.

DeLeo scanned the faces of everyone in the room. No one made a move, everyone listening, preparing for the worst.

"Wait!" Billy yelled and squirmed out of Ethel's arms. He ran into the darkness after them. In a flurry of panic, Ethel followed Billy, leaving DeLeo alone with Sadie.

Sadie smiled. "What a coincidence. It's just you and me now Wes. Close the vault," DeLeo froze. "Tell you what, I'll make it easier on you. I'll close it." Sadie walked toward the entrance.

"Sadie, did you plan all this?" DeLeo asked suspiciously, "to get them out of the vault?"

Sadie smirked, "I never kiss and tell."

A primal fear encompassed DeLeo at the thought that Sadie could be the craziest one here. This was his chance to get out and find the casino. It had to be close. He only had two options—risk it out there or stay in here with her.

DeLeo darted towards the door. Sadie tried to stop him but he pushed her to the ground and exited into the dark.

Wes moved quickly through the old bank. No sign of the others. They must be outside, he thought. He planned to sneak by John unnoticed, then pray to God he was going in the direction of the casino.

As DeLeo exited the bank, he heard a piercing scream. It sounded like Billy.

John had Tucker on his knees twenty feet away, curbside, his pistol pointed at the back of his head. The fog slowly snaked up their legs, putting them ankle-deep in white mist. Billy twisted in Ethel's grip, screaming for mercy for Tucker's life to be spared.

John's firearm exploded like a crack of lighting. Tucker fell forward disappearing into the fog. DeLeo could hear his body hit the asphalt with a soft thud.

He stood in horror at what had just happened. He had never seen anyone killed before, let alone shot in the head. Billy burst into tears and broke Ethel's strong grip, running to Tucker's aid.

DeLeo stood wide-eye watching Billy cradle Tucker's

dead body in his arms screaming.

"Sorry kid," John said. "You weren't supposed to see that."

"He's dead!" Billy cried. "He's dead and you killed him!!" Billy stared at John in disbelief.

"Quiet," John snapped. "Those fuckers are gonna hear you. Then we're all done for."

Billy made eye contact with DeLeo, then gently put Tucker's body back down in the fog. "Help me," he mouthed to DeLeo.

But DeLeo couldn't move. He didn't know what to do. He just wanted to be away from all of this.

Billy ran toward DeLeo embracing him, tears gushing down his face. "Help me. Take me away from this place. From these people. And take me away from HER," Billy sobbed, pointing at Ethel. Her hair was frazzled and red as blood.

Ethel grabbed Billy by the arm and ripped him off of DeLeo. "Get away from him," she hissed, spearing DeLeo with her eyes. "You're safe. You're safe with me Billy. John did what he had to do. Tucker was a monster — he needed to be stopped. A monster just like those demons. He would have turned on us, I know it. It was justice."

"Let's get back quick," Sadie whispered in DeLeo ear, startling him with her presence. She must have exited the bank unnoticed in all the commotion. "Just you and me. Those things will be here soon." Sadie tugged on his shirt, trying not to draw attention to them.

DeLeo started to back up, slowly. He could feel Sadie doing the same thing. John snapped to attention, quickly raising his pistol and pointing it at DeLeo. "Don't you go anywhere," John boomed. His brow glistened with sweat, his face seemed distorted, as if madness had finally taken hold of him. Reality seemed to have no meaning for him anymore.

"Why did you have to come here and ruin everything?" John's pistol hand shook as he spoke. A slight twitch interrupted the flow of his words. "Even if you didn't fuck her, I know you want to. I see the way you've been looking at her. It's the same way he looked at her," John said, tilting his head towards Tucker's limp body on the ground.

"John, there has to be rules." Ethel screamed, her nails digging into Billy's flesh as tried desperately to hold him back. "We need rules. How can a society function without rules? Shoot him. Shoot him in the head. He's a drug addict, a heathen, like all his kind."

"Shut the fuck up woman!" John screamed, momentarily taking his eyes off DeLeo to wipe the sweat from his face. "I can't just shoot everyone you don't like."

Out of the corner of his eye, DeLeo caught a blur of rage move past him. It was Sadie. She charged John and screamed, "I don't belong to you!" hitting him with so much force he dropped his gun.

DeLeo couldn't believe someone as petite as Sadie could move a man who was seemingly made of granite. As John regained his balance, a groan sounded in the fog, followed closely by another one.

Those things had returned, and they were close.

"You fool!" John hissed, searching for his gun in the knee-high fog. "Those things are close! Why did you do that?"

"I can take care of myself," Sadie shot back stubbornly.

Ethel let go of Billy, pushing Sadie aside to help John search for the gun.

"It has to be around here somewhere," John said pointing at the ground. "It can't be far."

Sadie looked to DeLeo, subtly nodding her head back at the bank. The groans grew closer and the fog thicker.

The unmistakable CLICK of a pistol stopped everyone in their tracks. Billy had found the gun and now stood pointing the firearm at John. Shaking, he held it with two hands, pointing it right at John. Surely, he was close enough not to miss.

John froze, slowly stood up, and put his hands out in front of him. "Billy, what are you doing? You don't want to hurt anyone, do you? Look. Ethel is right here."

"Why did you do it?" Billy asked gripping the pistol tighter in his hands. The fog had creeped up to his waist, the groans getting closer and closer. "Why did you kill him?"

"Billy, give John the gun, honey," Ethel pleaded in a soft, motherly tone. "He is only trying to protect us. Now, we need to get off the street and back into the vault before the demons come." Ethel swallowed hard, looked directly at Billy and stated, "Give him the gun."

"Don't call me Billy. " He looked at Ethel with disgust. "You're not even my mother. You can't tell me what to do."

"Please, Billy," John said. "Sorry, I mean Bill."

Billy persisted, moving forward, gun still drawn, his hands steady.

John snapped. "Give me the fuckin' gun, you little punk."

A mischievous smile appeared on Billy's face. "Like you said, without rules, there is only chaos." Without warning, Billy fired the weapon and before DeLco could scc what happened John's body disappeared into the fog.

"No!" Ethel screamed and tears flowed from her eyes as she rushed toward John.

Shocked, she stared open-mouthed at Billy. "What did you do?!"

"Stay away from me," Billy said backing away from Ethel. "I don't want you to touch me ever again. Ever!

You hear me?" Billy fired the gun again and Ethel's chest exploded as she slumped over into the fog.

Billy whipped the gun around, pointing it at Wes and Sadie. "Billy - Bill," Sadie corrected herself. "Put down the gun. Please," Sadie pleaded. The groans grew louder and more distinct. "We need to get off the street right now, it isn't safe out here."

Billy ignored her. Ignored the groans. "This is all your fault," he yelled, glaring at Sadie. "I saw what you did to Tucker. Even before he arrived," Billy continued, nodding towards DeLeo. "The eye contact, the smiles, the flirting. The touching here, the touching there. I saw it all. I saw what you did to him. You drove him to this. This is all your fault." Billy raised the gun.

There was something right behind him. DeLeo saw it — in the fog. It was one of those things. "And now you're going to die, just like him." Billy said.

Out of nowhere, a claw-like talon yanked Billy into the fog and DeLeo and Sadie could hear Billy screaming as he disappeared. The gun flashed as it fired rapidly in all directions, followed quickly by the agonizing cries of Billy being torn apart. The crack of bones, the ripping of flesh by what amounted to a savage pack of wolves.

All of a sudden, DeLeo noticed Sadie was no longer by his side. He heard labored breathing coming from the ground. It was Sadie, she had been hit by one of the bullets. She grabbed DeLeo by the shirt and coughed up blood. "The kid," she gasped, "I can't believe it. The kid. He shot me." Sadie started to shake, her eyes slowly rolling to the back of her head. The blood she coughed turned to a greenish foam.

"Sadie? Sadie?" DeLeo questioned again. He looked towards the fog where Billy had disappeared. It was silent except for the breathing of something waiting. One of those things? More figures started to take shape behind the fog and move closer.

Sadie began to shake in DeLeo arms. There was something different about her now. Her eyes were black, her skin now clammy to the touch.

What is this? DeLeo thought. He looked at her hands. Her nails were long and brown, like those things. His heart stopped.

Was she turning into one of those things?

DeLeo dropped Sadie to the ground as four of the beasts leaped out of the fog, their heads abnormally large, their mouthes tiny and beak-like, like an octopus or some sea-creature. Their eyes were huge, like bugs or even some cave-animal that had never seen the light of day. They towered over him, slimy, swaying, their chests heaving up and down, like a pack of hyenas ready to eat.

Sadie shook harder, spitting up more foam and mucus. DeLeo panicked, dropped her into the fog and ran.

His lungs burned as ran through the dark streets. He didn't dare look back at whatever those things were that remained. He could hear them, grunting, groaning, hissing, anything to get their claws on him.

DeLeo kept his hands out in front of him afraid some structure would pop up from the dark and knock him out leaving him for the beasts. DeLeo prayed the casino was just up ahead.

He passed the burnt, charred remains of what appeared to be an old Chevy truck. What seemed like traffic lights could be made out through the fog, dangling from a pole above. He came to an intersection but nothing looked familiar. Just keep moving he told himself. The casino had to be close.

Suddenly a flashing neon red blur appeared in the fog, then blue, and then yellow. That was it. The casino. It had to be. He ran harder, then tripped over something and fell to the ground, the palms of his hands scraping against the asphalt.

He tried to get to his feet and it was then that he felt it. Soft carpet rubbed the exposed cuts on his hands. It was the red carpet. He had tripped over one of the brass railings.

Excitement and hope overcame him. He was close but then again, so were those creatures. He quickly got to his feet and ran down the carpet, the neon rainbow colors of the sign coming into to focus:

"Endz Casino & Resort" sparkled and blazed in the night. Below, the revolving door slowly oscillated at the entrance, causing the fog to twist and swirl.

Running towards salvation, DeLeo hit the ground hard. Unseen and unheard, one of those things had jumped on his back. He turned to look, continuing to crawl back toward the door. It was Sadie, or whatever was left of her. Her face was contorted, her eyes black, her skin slimy and translucent. She made snapping, clicking sounds as she crawled across the ground toward him.

Behind her, DeLeo saw the shadows of what looked like a hoard of creatures. There had to be forty or fifty of them, maybe more.

The air had changed. It was warmer now, foul and wet, like rotting garbage. Sadie grabbed for DeLeo's foot. Her eyes hungry, her mouth drooling with thirst.

DeLeo kicked her off him and dove towards the revolving door. He knew this was it, this was his chance. He had to make it inside or the whole pack of creatures would tear him apart.

Safely inside the casino, he looked back through the glass, expecting those things to swarm in through the door and follow him inside. But they didn't. The door continued to turn easily but not one of the things even tried to enter. Instead, they smashed into the glass window, smudging it with their blood, mucus, and slime, licking the window like it was a lollipop.

"Welcome back, Sir," DeLeo heard a voice say from behind him. He turned and saw the Dealer standing behind the poker table, just like he had left him. "Don't worry," he said, casually shuffling a deck of cards, "You're safe in here. They can't get in."

DeLeo stood up and took a deep breath. "What the hell are those things?"

The Dealer raised one eyebrow, "People, just like you – or what's left of them. Lost souls. Shells of their former selves."

"Where the hell am I?" DeLeo exploded.

"Hell is a state of mind, Wes."

"No, No. I don't believe you. This isn't real. I don't belong here."

"No one does," the Dealer replied indifferently. "Are you ready to play now?" The Dealer placed his neatly shuffled deck of cards on the green felt of the poker table.

DeLeo looked back out the window. Those things were still licking and spitting on the window, smudging it with whatever foulness oozed from their pores.

Resigned, DeLeo dropped his shoulders, wiped the sweat off his face, and walked slowly towards the table. "I'm ready to play," he said, his voice barely a whisper.

"If I play, will you let me leave?" DeLeo sat at the poker table, his hands shaking, traumatized from what he just experienced.

"It's possible," the Dealer replied vaguely.

"I want to play. Let's just start now." DeLeo placed his arms on the green felt of the table. "What do I have to do?"

"Overcome a series of challenges," the Dealer said matter-of-factly. "But it will not be easy. You will have to confront things you might not be willing to accept."

DeLeo clasped his sweaty hands and looked the Dealer directly in the eyes.

"I'm ready."

The Dealer smiled for the first time, a mischievous, playful grin, and said, "You're in for a hell of a ride."

Turing away from DeLeo, the Dealer's voice took on a newfound charisma as he announced, "Welcome to It's Your Life!" His voice was newly amplified, joined by what sounded like an entire crowd of voices.

DeLeo shielded his eyes from the giant spotlights that

suddenly appeared from the ceiling. The walls around him rotated, revealing a studio audience and a production crew pointing cameras at his face.

Gone were the slot machines, craps tables, and bar. He was now standing in what appeared to be a TV studio. Bewildered, DeLeo looked at the Dealer. He was standing in front of him in a black bow-tie tuxedo, holding a long skinny microphone like Bob Barker on the Price is Right.

"Where are we?" the Dealer shouted into the microphone.

"It's Your Life!" the studio responded with cheers.

"That's right," the Dealer exclaimed, now all smiles. It was a complete transformation from what he had been before.

Confused and speechless, DeLeo could do nothing other than stand and stare like some awestruck animal caught in the headlights of a Mac truck right before getting sucked up into the wheel-well.

"I'm your host Chip Johnson," the Dealer continued, "and welcome to another episode of, It's Your Life,"

The Dealer, now Chip Johnson, walked toward the studio audience, with a bounce and pizazz of natural performer. "Do we have a great show for you or what? How about those special effects? Phenomenal right? And those performances?"

The crowd burst into applause. Chip flashed a smile for the first time. "We saw action, we saw horror, and was there more – a romance? Did we see a budding relationship or what?"

"Oooo!" the audience responded enthusiastically.

Chip paused on stage and turned toward DeLeo. "Look at him! Does he looked shocked or what?"

The hot glare of the light illuminated DeLeo. He stood alone, drenched in sweat on the opposite side of the stage.

He was in shock, disheveled, his eyes red, his hair a mess. Chip raced across the stage and shoved the long pencil thin microphone in his face.

"How do you feel Wes?"

The audience went silent, the cameras zoomed in for the dramatic reveal. Chip inched the mic forward. "Wes," Chip said tilting the microphone away from his mouth for a moment. "The audience and the people watching at home want to know how you feel."

"Is this real?" DeLeo finally managed to get out. His words echoed across the stage.

Chip burst into laughter, "Of course it's real," he said into the microphone. "Let's give Mr. DeLeo a few moments to catch his breath, while we get caught up." Chip pointed to three giant LCD screens lowered from the ceiling.

The studio went dark. Areal footage of a nameless, rough desert landscape appeared on screen, accompanied by a thick, gravely, movie trailer voice. "Coming to you live. Deep in the desert of an undisclosed location comes the groundbreaking new show, It's Your Life."

Just as the narrator dramatically stated the name of the show a large, arena-sized dome appeared in the middle of the desert.

"What is this?" DeLeo said to Chip, his eyes fixated on the screens. The areal footage faded to black and suddenly the footage was inside the arena. Dark buildings and the burnt out remains of cars were scattered throughout an apocalyptic city. The aerial drone footage moved through the fog until the glowing neon sign appeared reading:

Endz Casino & Resort.

Chip leaned over to DeLeo, "I told you, you're in for a hell of a ride."

Handheld footage of DeLeo singing and playing acoustic guitar at dive bar appeared. DeLeo instantly remembered the venue. That's the place he was right before he woke up here.

"Shots," a female voice said behind the camera. The bartender made the drink and handed it to the person wearing the camera, who took out two small pills and put them in the glass where they instantly dissolved on contact with the liquid. The person stirred the shot with a straw and turned to the mirror behind the bar. It was Sadie. She was wearing a small camera hidden in her glasses. She winked and smiled at her reflection.

The audience gasped, then chuckled.

DeLeo remained confused as he watched the footage of Sadie fixing her stylish overly-sized glasses, then moved through the empty bar. DeLeo saw himself come into frame and watched as Sadie handed him the drink and he gulped it down.

The footage jumped ahead. Sadie was out in the parking lot. DeLeo watched himself burst out of one of the back doors and vomit in the bushes. His eyes rolled back, and he dropped to the ground.

A nearby van door opened and six people dressed in white coats carrying a stretcher emerged. DeLeo watched the group of white coats pick him off the ground, and take off in the van.

"You did great," a voice said from off screen.

Sadie moved her head, turning the camera to reveal Chip Johnson stepping out of a black town car.

DeLeo watched the footage cut to the casino floor, and the same six white-coats prop him up on a chair in front of the poker table. DeLeo slowly woke up asking, "Where am I?"

The screens went black and the TV monitors retracted into the ceiling.

"How about that?" Chip asked the audience who burst

into applause, laughing. "Now, that you've had time to take it all in Wes, what do you think?"

The microphone now inches from DeLeo mouth, "I'm on a TV show?" he said, barely able to speak. "None of it was real?"

"Nope," Chip said, flashing a mouth full of white veneers the size of chiclets. "But it takes a village, so first let us bring out our amazingly talented actors."

The audience whistled and applauded with anticipation.

"First let us meet our zany zealot, religious fundamentalist, overprotective mother figure. You know her as Ethel — Jane Fern."

DeLeo watched as Ethel, or the person he had know as Ethel, walked through the revolving door behind him. She smiled and waved at the crowd. She paraded herself in front of the audience, her blouse still covered in red. DeLeo now assumed was just fake blood. Ethel stopped on the opposite side of Chip and smiled at the audience.

"Next," Chip continued. "The dangerously deviant, fraternizing frat boy, you know him as Tucker — Shawn Blaine."

Tucker walked through the revolving door waving to the crowd. His face was red, hair dried and matted with fake blood. After waving to the audience, he stopped next to Ethel. "Next up, the darkhorse — who saw that coming?" Chip laughed. "I see a future Academy Award on his shelf. The next DiCaprio or Pacino dare I say. You know him as Billy, or should I say, Bill." The audience broke into laughter. Billy emerged through the revolving door performing a cartwheel, then back handspring. The crowd erupted into enthusiastic applause. Billy finished his entrance by blowing kisses at the teenage girls in the front row.

"Every story can only be as good as its villain. And boy did we have a hell of a good bad guy right?" The cheers of the audience were only white noise to DeLeo now. He was still in disbelief from people he watched die violent deaths suddenly emerge through the revolving door with smiles on their faces.

"Let me ask you this," Chip asked the crowd, now talking to the audience like they were the best of friends, "why is the practical one, with the street smarts, and leadership qualities always the villain? What a cliche. All he wanted to do was keep everyone safe — go figure. You know him as rough and tough bad cop John, but please welcome, from across the pond—why are they always British? Rupert B. Chamberlain."

John walked out of the revolving doors. Gone were his strong American-macho gestures as he fawned at the audience. Replaced by effeminate smiles, batting eyelashes and an unimposing posture, he humbly took his place between Tucker and Billy on the line.

"Am I missing someone?" Chip yelled to the audience.

"Yes!" they shouted when he pointed the microphone at them.

"Oh yes, how could I forget? What would a story be without the foxy fun, beautiful but deadly femme fatal? You know her as Sexy Sadie—was she good or what? Everyone give it up for Sarah Charles!"

Sadie walked through the revolving doors to a standing ovation. Covered in slime and fake blood she smiled like a prom queen.

"What was it like working with this team of amazingly talented actors?" Chip asked Sadie.

"Um," Sadie paused, thinking out loud, smiling and chomping down on a piece of gum. "It's always like a challenge. These guys and gals were, like, so great though! Like true professionals. And I would like work with them any day."

"Thanks, darling," Chip kissed her on the cheek and tapped her on the butt. "And of course, we can't forget our disgusting, horrible monsters and our wonderful special effects team."

One by one, slimy reptilian monsters walked through the revolving door. DeLeo was growing more furious by the minute, imagining some asshole underneath all that make-up grinning in his suit. He watched as the monsters lined up next to the actors like it was all a joke. He felt a deep swelling hatred brewing within him.

The spotlight returned to DeLeo followed immediately by Chip's long thin microphone. "Now that you've had a bit of time for all that to sink in Wes, how do you feel?"

DeLeo glared at the group of actors on the other side of Chip Johnson, or whatever his name was. He could feel his shock and anger boiling over. Then slowly leaned into the microphone and growled, "I'm going to fucking kill you."

7

Chip Johnson pulled the microphone away from DeLeo. "Well how about that? Live TV, you can't predict what will happen, but this is a family show. Anyway, we'll be right back after a few words from our sponsors."

"And we're clear," a cameraman said from a sea of crew underneath a large LCD screen showing that the broadcast had gone to commercial.

Chip let out a gasp and dropped his shoulders. A makeup artist ran out and dabbed the sweat from his face. Suddenly, DeLeo felt someone touching his face. It was another makeup artist.

"What the hell are you doing?" DeLeo pushed the young woman away from him.

"Sorry sir," she replied frightened, "but if I don't touch up the sweat, it will glisten on camera. It won't look good."

"Relax Wes," said Chip. "It's just TV buddy. She's trying to make you look good."

"Look good?" DeLeo exploded. "I'm going to sue the shit out of you." DeLeo turned to the actors, who were gossiping amongst themselves while makeup artists touched up shiny faces and smoothed hair. "You were all in on this?" he shouted.

The group of actors glanced at each other, seeming to wait for someone else to speak. "We're actors mate," John said raising his eyebrows and forcing a smile.

"You better lawyer up. All of you," DeLeo snapped. "This is how you ruin someone's life!"

"Come on Wes," Sadie said, her smile sweet like the first time he saw her. "We're artists," she continued.

"Con artists," DeLeo hollered.

"Chill out man," Tucker said. "We're just doing our job."

"We just want to help you Wes," Sadie added.

"Help me?" DeLeo burst into a rage. He couldn't hold his anger back anymore. "How are you trying to help me?"

In a fury, DeLeo flipped over the poker table in front of him. It crashed to the ground startling everyone in the studio. Whispers in the audience were followed by a nervous tension filling the room.

Two security guards rushed toward the stage. Chip put his hands out motioning toward them that he would take care of DeLeo. A moment later, after the guards returned to their positions behind the crew, Chip cautiously approached DeLeo.

"Just relax Wes," Chip said calmly, trying to talk sense into him. "You're only making a fool out of yourself on live TV. Plus you're destroying private property, so we're going to have to charge you for that."

In disbelief, DeLeo scanned the blank, frightened faces in the crowd, all staring at him with judging, nervous eyes. DeLeo breathed slowly calming himself down. There was no sense in getting angry here. It wouldn't prove anything. He would only end up looking crazy on national TV.

DeLeo tried to think of positive thoughts. If it was all

fake, maybe he could go home and sleep in his bed tonight. DeLeo straightened himself up, took a deep breath and said, "Chip, so that's your name?"

"That's right buddy," Chip flashed a great big phony smile.

"As soon as this whole thing is over," DeLeo started, grinning back at him, "I'll be getting my lawyer, but until then I'll play along." DeLeo let the makeup woman dab the sweat from his face without protest.

"We're back on in 10!" a crew member yelled from behind the camera, and pointed to Chip, "in 5, 4, 3, 2," he motioned the number 1 with his finger.

Chip addressed the camera. "Welcome back after that quick commercial break. Now, the big news everyone has been waiting for, the romance between Sadie and Wes. Let's look at the footage."

The studio went dark. The monitors hanging from the ceiling showed a quick montage of DeLeo and Sadie entering the vault and meeting the survivors. The footage cut forward to them talking, and then finally to them heading to their corners for bed.

Sadie crouched down in front of DeLeo. "You know," Sadie whispered. "If you want you can come to my corner."

DeLeo played along and smiled watching the interaction between him and Sadie on the TV screen. He remembered what happened, but it was still strange watching such an intimate moment on large screens with a crowd. The video cut forward in time.

DeLeo watched Sadie curl up next to him under the blanket. There was movement, and the sound of kissing, but not the words said between the two, namely DeLeo rejecting Sadie's advances. DeLeo couldn't believe it. That wasn't what had happened. It looked as though they were having sex on the screen.

"This isn't right. That didn't happen." DeLeo said aloud. His words went unnoticed, overpowered by the "ooo's" and "awe's of the studio audience.

DeLeo ran to Chip, "What are you doing to me? This isn't real. This never happened. Not like this."

The footage stopped. The spotlight returned to Chip and DeLeo standing on stage. DeLeo's face pale. Beads of sweat glistened in the hot studio light.

Chip smiled at the audience, "Looks like we hit a nerve huh?"

The crowd laughed. Chip slowly walked toward Sadie, ignoring DeLeo. "What do you think of that?" he asked her.

Sadie's gum popped, amplified by the speakers. She spoke out of the corner of her mouth taking big juicy chomps between every word. "I think he's, like, cute," Sadie said with a big smile, "but, um, how do I say it. He's not my type. Tell you the truth it was a bit awkward. However, I'm a professional, so I, um, went along with it." Sadie flashed the audience a bright smile and they cheered.

"Wow honey, you are a natural! Able to improvise at the drop of a hat. Let me ask you this, maybe you weren't into him, but was he into you? If you know what I mean?" Chip winked. The audience chuckled.

Sadie giggled, "I think he was."

"This is bullshit!" DeLeo screamed. He wanted to push her and punch Chip's grin into the back of his face.

Chip laughed, "Oh to be young and in love. The passion, the anger, it's all coming out now." Chip turned to DeLeo and grinned. "But what about DeLeo's wife — where does she fit into all of this?"

DeLeo froze.

A shocked gasp radiated throughout the studio. Chip

waved his arms to silence the crowd. Suddenly the studio returned to the same quiet DeLeo remembered when he first woke up. The low hum of the ventilation system. The audience waited in suspense.

The lights dimmed. Chip pointed to a dark window at the base of the stage. "Let us look inside door number one." Inside the window, a light turned on and there she was, the love of Wes DeLeo's life, his wife, Amber. She looked sad, embarrassed, alone. Next to her was DeLeo's young daughter, Delilah, holding a small Elmo doll, a look of confusion plastered across her innocent face.

"How are you holding up?" Chip asked, looking across the stage to Amber.

"I'm doing okay. I guess," Amber responded slowly from behind the glass without raising her head.

Chip approached the small window where Amber stood with Delilah. "What do you have to say about seeing your husband behaving like that with Sadie?"

Amber raised her head. Sadness and pain beamed from her eyes. "I'm hurt and disappointed," Amber said. "I always knew Wes was someplace else. Like he wasn't really present when he was with me, but I thought it was his music. It was always his music, chasing his big dream of becoming a famous musician. I never thought there would be another woman. Seeing the video with him and Sadie proves that things were worse than I thought they were."

"It's not true," DeLeo cried. Tears flowed from his eyes. "They're lying. I didn't touch her. I've always been faithful to you."

Before DeLeo could speak, Amber spoke again, "One time he came home smelling of perfume. I asked him about it, but he said it was nothing and changed the subject."

"That was from a show," DeLeo pleaded. "I can't help people coming up to me. It's not true!"

Chip chided DeLeo like a father to a son, "As a thirty-five-year-old man should you really be out all night chasing the dreams of a twenty-five-year-old? At your age, still having delusions of becoming a rock star, is well, a little pathetic am I right?"

The audience erupted in support of Chip Johnson.

Chip gently touched DeLeo's shoulder. "Wes, here's your chance to get the record straight. The whole country is watching."

DeLeo wiped the tears from his face. "We were having trouble. That's true. I moved out, but I didn't cheat on her. I didn't do anything wrong."

"What do you think Sadie?" Chip asked her as she quietly gossiped with the cast. "Are Wes's emotions real?"

Sadie faced the crowd like she was about to give a performance, "Let me tell you Chip, I'm, like, an actor, so I know when other people are lying and let me tell you, Wes DeLeo is a terrific actor."

"No, I'm telling the truth," DeLeo said to Amber. Fresh tears ran down his face. "I love you. I know we've had problems but you're everything to me." Amber stood in silence, not uttering a word as DeLeo pleaded for forgiveness.

"Wes, sometimes saying less is actually saying more," Sadie announced to the audience cutting off his cries for redemption.

"Shut up!" DeLeo screamed at her.

The audience gasped. DeLeo quickly realized his outburst was inappropriate, "I'm sorry. I didn't mean that. I'm just confused. It's this show. Please, Amber, believe me. I don't know what is going on."

"Blaming the victim," Sadie sighed, "have you ever taken responsibility for anything Wes DeLeo?"

"Amber, any final comments?" Chip asked into the microphone. His voice was soft and gentle.

"I tried. I really did." Amber hugged Delilah who stood at her side. "I hope Wes can get the help he needs. For our daughter's sake."

"Thank you Amber" Chip said. "I know that was difficult, but you're a stronger woman for it."

"Give it up for Amber!" Sadie cheered. The audience applauded, and the light in the window faded down.

Amber and Delilah were gone.

"What are you doing to me?" DeLeo asked.

Chip brought the microphone to his face, "Wes, you're in good hands now. We're not going to let you down. Just think about your daughter, your wife. We're going to get you the help you need. Aren't we?" Chip said addressing the audience.

"Yes!" the crowded yelled in unison.

"I can't hear you!" Chip said putting his hand behind his ear.

"Yes!" the enthusiastic group chanted again, this time joined by the cast and crew.

"Good. We all want the same thing for Wes here. That's why we got the best in the business. Give it up for Dr. Helen Stone."

Helen Stone clumsily walked on to the stage, her ankles bending above her chunky, scuff marked heels. She wore glasses and a tweed coat, resembling something of a 1950's librarian. Shc wavcd to the audience, then rubbed DeLeo on the back for support as a mother does her child.

"Thank you for a wonderful show," Chip announced. "We'll see you next time on…" Chip put his hand behind his ear signaling to the crowd.

The audience yelled enunciating every syllable, "It's Your Life!"

Two large men wearing white coats, who looked like

hospital orderlies, approached DeLeo and gently clasped him by the arms. "What are you doing?" DeLeo asked confused.

"Just a precaution sir," one of the white coats said.

"Precaution for what?"

"You're in good hands Wes," Dr. Helen Stone said, adding her support. "This is a full-fledged medical facility. We're going to take good care of you. Think of your daughter."

"When do I get to go home?" DeLeo asked Dr. Stone. The cheering crowd was still so loud he was almost unable to hear himself speak.

"These things take time, but we'll have you fixed up and back to your family soon. These men will take good care of you until our first session later."

The monotonous drone of smooth jazz greeted DeLeo when he entered the elevator just off the studio floor. The two white coats still had a firm grip on his arms.

DeLeo wasn't going to run, at least not now. He was too exhausted. The end of the episode had been a fast blur, and the hysterical laughing and cheering of the audience still lingered in his ears. The Red Scare tactics and witch trial accusations had worked. He was beaten. Tired.

Gone was the anger and fury. It had been replaced by subtle elevator jazz, just audible enough to make him want a warm shower and bed.

One of the orderlies pushed floor thirty on the elevator panel. A soft soothing click followed, then the smooth elevator hum of the iron box going up. To where, DeLeo had no clue and at the moment, he didn't care.

Moments later the elevator door opened with a ding. The two men escorted DeLeo into an empty room that appeared to be a reception area in a doctor's office. It smelled vaguely of disinfectant and baby wipes.

"Please sit," the receptionist said from behind her glass window.

"Where am I?" DeLeo responded. The woman ignored DeLeo and slid the glass shut.

DeLeo glanced at one of the white coats for an answer, but they both had returned to the elevator, which abruptly closed behind them.

The pleather reception area couch squeaked when De-Leo sat down. Gossip magazines were spread out across the coffee table. Internet celebrities and new popstars decorated the pages. People DeLeo didn't recognize and didn't care to. His days of keeping up with the hot new trends were gone. He inspected the plastic shoulder-height plant next to the couch then shut his eyes.

After dozing for a minute or two, DeLeo walked across the room to a small window that looked outside. It was night. His eyes adjusted to the darkness, and suddenly he realized he was looking out on the set of the post-apoca-lyptic cityscape from the TV show. The fog was gone, but he knew for sure it was the same city. Below he saw peo-ple who appeared to be janitors or set designers hosing off what looked like fake blood and slime.

He chuckled. He still couldn't believe everything he went through was just a TV show.

"Mr. DeLeo," the receptionist said from behind him, "Dr. Stone will see you now."

DeLeo pointed out the window, "are they getting it ready for the next victim?"

"Contestant," the receptionist said defensively, then pointed to a door next to the reception window.

As DeLeo walked toward the door, he noticed a camera in the top corner of the room. It was painted the same egg-shell color white as the rest of the wall, he assumed to try and disguise it from wandering eyes or suckers like himself. Someone was watching him right now. Probably the Dealer, or Chip — whatever his name was.

DeLeo entered the door and walked down a quiet, narrow hallway until he came to another door. He had no idea what to expect or what this doctor was going to try to tell him. The anger started to return, bubbling to the surface like a volcano. DeLeo paused. Get a hold of yourself he thought. He took a deep breath and knocked on the door, which slowly swung open.

Dr. Stone stood behind a massive mahogany desk and greeted DeLeo with a firm handshake. She was tall and lanky. DeLeo noticed right away that her clothes were too big for her, like giant bags on her small frame.

"Please sit," Dr. Stone pointed to a brown leather armchair opposite her desk. Books and old papers cluttered the small office. A computer sat untouched in the corner.

As DeLeo sat in the chair, he eyed the corners of the room, trying to find the cameras, which were obviously there.

"I take it this is being recorded?" DeLeo snapped, not bothering to hide his annoyance.

Dr. Stone ignored his question and reached for a clipboard amongst all the clutter on her desk. She leaned back in her chair and used a chewed pen to navigate her notes. "Wes DeLeo: addict, adulterer, absentee father," she paused and made eye contact with DeLeo for the first time.

"All lies," he said.

DeLeo knew she was fishing for a reaction, and so were the cameras. He wasn't going to give her the satisfaction of losing his temper. He sat there like a slab of granite.

Dr. Stone changed her posture, "But it seems you do have some redeeming qualities," she continued, "you're a musician. Quite a good one too it seems." DeLeo didn't respond. A slight scowl came over Dr. Stone's face, "but it seems like you wasted that talent as well."

DeLeo burst into laughter, "is this what they teach you at therapy school? To insult the patient?"

"I'm only trying to understand."

"Then try to understand how messed up all of this is. This show, intervention, whatever it is you think you're doing."

"I want to talk about your music."

"Fine. What about?"

"It's tough getting older isn't it?"

"Huh?"

"We all have dreams Wes. We all think we're going to grow up and be something special: a famous movie star, a writer, a musician, the leader of a movement, a revolutionary, the president. It's tough when those things don't come true, isn't it? And life just moves on. It's tough to watch yourself age out of the role you always imagined for yourself."

DeLeo gripped the leather armchair, "What are you getting at?"

"No matter how many clubs you play, how many songs you write, how many hours you practice, sometimes it just doesn't happen. That disillusion can lead to anger or resentment and play itself out in other areas of your life. Like your family."

DeLeo didn't want to talk anymore. He returned to his original plan of absolute silence.

After a minute of quiet, Dr. Stone spoke, "I can't help if you don't talk to me. Where is your mind wandering off to Wes? Are you angry with my questions? Can you tell me about your daughter? You wife?" Dr. Stone put down the clipboard and stared at DeLeo. After a long, silent moment, her soft tone turned to contempt. "Mr. DeLeo, I don't think you understand. I can play the silent game all day, all week, or all month. It's up to you. You were signed into my custody. Yes this may be a television show, but I am a licensed psychiatrist, and you're not leaving this facility without my approval."

DeLeo leaned forward, "What are you talking about?"

"We'll talk later." Dr. Stone hit the intercom in her desk, "Hector, Mr. DeLeo is ready to be shown to his quarters."

Four orderlies entered the room. The biggest one, the leader, was clearly Hector

"Wait, I want to see a lawyer," DeLeo said backing against the wall.

"Mr. DeLeo, remember you are in my custody. If you don't behave, we will have to sedate you," Dr. Stone said calmly.

"What the fuck are you talking about?"

"Hector, please remove Mr. DeLeo from my office."

DeLeo tried to dodge the white coats but smashed up against Hector.

"We can do this the easy way or the hard way," Hector said, nodding to one of the other orderlies, "Show Mr. De-Leo his options."

The white coat raised his arms to show a syringe in one hand and a straight jacket in the other.

"I'm fine," DeLeo adjusted his shoulders. "I can walk. Just show me to my room."

Hector and the others escorted Wes down the narrow hallway until they came to an open railing that looked down on to what appeared to be a hotel courtyard ten floors below. The white noise of conversations mixed with the sophisticated sound of live jazz piano and clinking glasses radiated from below.

DeLeo looked over the edge. People were dressed in their best formal wear. Tuxedos, gowns designed by the best designers. Waiters held trays of shrimp cocktail, bacon wrapped scallops, and champagne. Suddenly someone caught DeLeo's eye. He squinted to make sure what he saw was real. Amongst the crowd, DeLeo saw Sadie, Ethel, John, and the rest of the cast and crew from before.

"What is this?" DeLeo asked Hector, confused.

"The after party," Hector pulled DeLeo into an elevator.

This elevator was different from the one before. Made of glass and operating on the inside of the building, DeLeo could see the party below as they ascended. He watched Sadie sip wine and flirt with other beautiful people. She dazzled, like she was dressed for the Academy Awards.

DeLeo clenched his fists. He felt like everything that was happening was at his expense. Like they were praising his demise. His loss. Moreover, they were celebrating. Partying, laughing, at the destruction of Wes DeLeo.

The elevator came to a stop. Hector and the orderlies steered DeLeo down another narrow hallway, this one filled with numbered doors. Hector opened one of the entries with a key. The lights automatically turned on when they entered. It was a small room with plain walls, a bed, and television. A divider curtain separated the bedroom from the small bathroom. On the bed were a set of clean clothes and a tray with a hot meal on it.

"Rest up," Hector stated. "Tomorrow's a big day."

"What happens tomorrow?"

The door shut and DeLeo heard a lock from the other side. Stunned, he grabbed the doorknob. Those bastards had locked him inside. DeLeo promptly moved around the room checking every corner and bedpost for a camera or microphone. He found nothing.

DeLeo ate, showered, then lay on the bed. He was exhausted. Tomorrow was another day. He turned on the TV. They were airing his episode of, It's Your Life.

DeLeo watched himself as he first exited Endz Casino,

a look of confusion on his face. He wondered if that same look was on his face now. He changed the channel. It was the after party from the courtyard below. Sadie, John, Chip they were all there. Laughing.

Rage shot through his system like an electrical surge. Frozen to the TV screen, he couldn't change the channel. DeLeo turned up the sound. The whole cast was there, standing by the bar, cleaned up and dressed in their best evening attire. "Did you see when his wife showed up?" Sadie said bursting into laughter. She twisted the stem of her crystal wine glass. "The look on his face was price-less."

"Just amazing, spectacular TV," Tucker responded. "Who says the Golden Age is over?"

"We don't get those type of moments in the U.K.," John added through a posh British accent while eyeing the ass of a young male waiter.

"I'll have one of those," Billy said emerging from the crowd and taking two glasses off the waiter's tray.

"What do you think you're doing young man?" Sadie said to Billy, "You're barely old enough to drive, let alone drink."

Billy smiled and handed Sadie one of the glasses, "I'm old enough for you."

"Honey please," Sadie took the glass out of Billy's hand.

"Lighten up," Ethel said. "Let the kid have a little fun."

"Who are you calling a kid," Billy said offended, "I'm old enough for you too."

Ethel grinned, "That so? You wouldn't know what to do with me."

"I have a few ideas," Billy winked and took two fresh glasses of champagne off the tray, nodded at a few teenage girls, and disappeared into the crowd.

DeLeo shut off the TV and threw the controller at the

wall. The remote exploded into a million pieces. Plastic shards sprayed in every direction.

DeLeo paced the small room. All he could think about were those liars downstairs mocking him. Manipulating his thoughts. He tried to open the door.

Locked.

He slammed his body against it. Nothing. He ripped the TV off the wall and slammed it into the ground. He tried to flip the bed over, but it was bolted to the floor.

DeLeo collapsed on the floor in tears. He was alone. The thought of being stuck in this room, away from his family forever, began to seep into his mind. He had never cheated on his wife. Selfish, yes, but unfaithful—no.

Suddenly there was a soft knock at the door. At first, DeLeo didn't think anything of it; he must have been hearing things. Then it happened again. He sat up and looked at the door.

Was someone there?

A key slid under the small gap between the floor and the bottom of the door. Someone was trying to help.

DeLeo waited a moment before retrieving it. Seconds later he put the key into the doorknob, half expecting it not to work.

The lock clicked. The door opened.

"Hello?" DeLeo whispered into the hall. There was no response. Whoever had helped him was already gone.

DeLeo moved cautiously down the hallway, his eyes darting from corner to ceiling looking for cameras. In the pit of his stomach, he expected Hector or one of the other orderlies to jump out from behind a door and tackle him.

DeLeo peered over the edge of the railing into the courtyard, making sure only his eyes were visible. The party was still raging below. The guests were louder now and probably drunk.

DeLeo entered the same glass elevator he had ridden up in and pushed L for lobby. He made sure to stay away from the glass, hugging the door, so no one from the party would see him.

A sense of relief came over DeLeo when the elevator door opened into an empty hallway rather than the crowded courtyard floor. The corridor was clear. The sound of corks popping and drunken conversation drifted from the nearby party.

Suddenly DeLeo froze at the sound of laughter. Someone was near. Close. DeLeo noticed a restroom a few doors down and ran toward it. His heart raced, thumping in his chest as he slipped through the swinging door. DeLeo quickly looked under the bathroom stalls. It was empty.

Someone from outside chuckled again. It was a familiar sound. DeLeo had heard it before. Curiosity got the best of him, and he slowly peered out the restroom door. It was Billy with a girl on his arm and they were coming near him, toward the restroom.

DeLeo closed the door softly and darted to the end stall. Once inside he locked it and stood on the toilet in case they looked under.

The main door open. Billy entered with his girl. "Come on," he heard Billy say. "There's no one in here, it's just you and me. We'll have a little fun."

DeLeo held his breath as Billy brought the girl into the next stall. He waited until he heard them getting lost in the moment—kissing, belts coming off, zippers going down. The movements and groans of passion filled the small restroom.

DeLeo lightly put his foot on the ground and slowly unlocked his stall. Part of DeLeo wanted to kick down Billy's stall door and beat the shit out of him for what he did. However, he was still just a kid, and of all of the cast Billy was the one he hated the least.

DeLeo exited the restroom and continued down the corridor. He slowed down when he approached the courtyard entrance. Through a set of French doors with golden handles, he could see into the ballroom. There were easily a hundred people inside, partying, drinking, celebrating at his expense. Busy waiters made their way to and from the kitchen and the bar. Money was clearly not a problem for whoever was paying for this party.

DeLeo caught Sadie moving about the party seducing everyone she talked to. A knot formed in his stomach. He clenched his jaw. He wanted to talk to her. Ask her a few questions. Get some answers.

Truthfully he wanted to scream in her face. Make her feel the pain she made him feel. His fists tightened. He wanted to hit something as hard as he could. Destroy something. Make what was once beautiful ugly.

Sadie kissed Chip Johnson on each side of his cheek, then Tucker, and finally John, as if she was saying good-bye. She was leaving DeLeo thought. This was a perfect time to get her alone and talk to her.

DeLeo observed Sadie like a lion stalks its prey. From the crack through the French doors no one saw him. His eyes raised to the top of his lids, his head slightly pointed down. He just wanted to talk to her. Ask a few questions. That was it.

Sadie headed toward the exit. DeLeo was patient. When she stepped out into the hallway. DeLeo kept his distance, ducking in doorways and behind large tropical plants scattered along the corridor for decoration. He wanted to talk to her someplace quiet. Away from all these people.

Sadie turned a corner. DeLeo waited then followed. Sadie's ankle buckled form her massive heels. She must be drunk, DeLeo thought. Too much Sauvignon Blanc. Up ahead he saw a maintenance closet. This was his moment.

DeLeo crept up silently from behind and without sound or warning, grabbed her. He put a hand over her mouth and with the other locked her arms close to her body. "Don't move," he whispered in her ear. Her body tensed. He could feel her fear. Her muscles twitched. Her neck tightened as he dragged her into the maintenance closet.

The closet was dark and musty, lit by one lone bulb above. Mops and cleaning supplies lined the walls, along with toilet paper and room-ready shampoos and conditions.

"Please don't hurt me!" Sadie cried as DeLeo flipped her

around.

"Shut up," he said. The fury bubbling to the surface. "You know how to mess with a person's mind, don't you? You destroyed my life. Made a fool out of me. I don't want to hurt you. I want to kill you." He pushed her to the ground. "I want you to feel the same pain you made me feel."

"I'll scream," Sadie said behind frightened eyes.

DeLeo grabbed her by the neck and began to squeeze. "I'm not going to let you do that."

Sadie wiggled, trying everything to move from his grip. Finally, she broke free and backed against the closet wall. "Please, this is just a show. It's all fake. Please."

DeLeo moved closer.

"Help," she yelled again, pulling out what appeared to be a microphone from her dress. "Help," she yelled again. "Bravo, bravo, I want out."

DeLeo pulled the microphone out of her hand. A long cord ran into a transmitter hidden under her dress.

"What the hell is this?" DeLeo yelled.

"It's all fake," Sadie pleaded. "The key? Who do you think let you out of your room?"

Suddenly the door burst opened and a group of heavily armed men wearing blue SWAT uniforms entered. They wore face masks and held batons. DeLeo swung violently at whoever tried to touch him.

"Take him down," a voice outside the closet yelled.

In a moment DeLeo was pinned against the ground. Out of the corner of his eye he saw Hector enter the closet with a large syringe in his hand. He felt a sting in his arm and everything went black.

10

DeLeo woke to white fluorescent lights overhead and his arms and legs shackled to a chair. His ribs hurt, probably from one of the roided-out orderlies or the fascist SWAT team. Why would a TV show need a souped-up security force like that?

In front of DeLeo was a windowless door cut into a cement wall and a large LCD screen. A closed-circuit camera buzzed in the top corner of the cell pointing right at him. DeLeo screamed at the camera, pulling at the chains on his arms and feet.

The TV monitor then faded up from black showing footage of what happened after he was sedated. DeLeo watched as the security force left. Sadie stood up and fixed her dress. Hector and the other white coats prepared to take his unconscious body away.

"Wait," Sadie said to Hector, who was preparing to move DeLeo's sedated body. Now shackled to the chair, DeLeo watched Sadie kick him as hard as she could in the stomach. DeLeo instantly thought of the pain in his side and knew where it came from.

"Are you okay?" Chip said to Sadie walking into frame.

"Do I look okay?" she snapped back.

"We were just waiting for you to give us the signal."

"I tried to give you the signal, but his damn hand was around my throat!" Sadie ripped off the remainder of the microphone wire and handed it to Chip. "I thought no one was supposed to get hurt. This guy is dangerous! I'm just an actor."

"Are you okay?" Ethel asked, out of breath from running to the scene of the incident. John entered right behind, breathing heavily. "I heard what happened and I came right away."

"I'm fine," Sadie said annoyed. Chip helped her out of the closet.

"All the excitement is over," Chip said to the cast. "Please go back to the party. Enjoy yourself. We'll take care of this."

"You sure?" Ethel asked.

"Yes, I'm fine." Sadie said, "Go on, head back."

Chip waited for the cast to leave before he kissed Sadie. Shackled to the chair Wes watched the two on screen, it seemed as though they had a previous relationship. But Wes's mind was foggy and it was tough to tell what was real and what was fake.

"Chip, don't smile at me like that." Sadie said, the corner of her mouth turning into a grin. "I mean, this guy is seriously messed up. He snapped for Christ sakes. Some people can't be rehabilitated."

"I'm sorry, it got a little out of hand," Chip said, "I take full responsibility. I didn't mean to put you in that type of position."

Sadie smiled coyly. "You know, you're a jerk sometimes Chip. I might have to talk to my union rep."

Chip pouted his lips, "You wouldn't do that, would you? We're making television history!"

"You're still a jerk," Sadie brushed a piece of her hair behind her ear.

Chip pulled Sadie close to him and kissed her, "Is this something a bottle of wine can fix?"

"I'm not that easy?"

"Really?" Chip smiled. "Aren't all actresses that easy?"

"Shut up," Sadie laughed, feigning outrage, and kissed Chip again. "Let's go have that bottle of wine."

DeLeo watched the two of them walk down the hallway, Chip's arm around Sadie's shoulder. Then the camera cut to himself drooling unconsciously as Hector and the orderlies wheeled him in the opposite direction. The screen faded to black.

The cell door unlocked and the door swung open. Dr. Stone entered the interrogation room with Hector by her side.

DeLeo immediately applauded their entrance, his chains rattling as his hands barely reached together. "Bravo, bravo. You guys are such geniuses."

Dr. Stone stared at Hector, confused, then approached DeLeo. Without taking her eyes off of her clipboard, she said, "You attacked one of the actors."

"Just a stunt. None of it was real. It's TV." DeLeo laughed. "Remember? Am I right Hector? What are you an ex-wrestler or something? You look like it."

Dr. Stone looked into DeLeo's eyes. "You're wrong about that. After your actions in the closet, your wife had you officially committed. You're lucky Sarah isn't pressing charges."

"Sarah? I'm still going to still call her Sadie. And her pressing charges? I should be the one pressing charges! I want to speak with my wife."

"I'm afraid that's out of the question. The decisions you made got you here Mr. DeLeo, and it will be the decisions you make from now on that will get you out of here — if that time ever comes."

"This can't be legal."

"I can assure it is. You are a danger to yourself and, as the video showed, you are a danger to others as well. We are fully committed to your recovery. It's our job to help rehabilitate you with whatever means possible. We don't want you to relapse like so many do."

"Fuck you!" DeLeo yelled and pulled at his chains.

"If you don't remain calm, I'll have Hector sedate you."

"I want out," DeLeo screamed into the camera, then spit on Dr. Stone.

Dr. Stone shook her head in disapproval then looked at the cameras in the corner of the cell as if to ask permission for her next move. "Hector, please see to it that Mr. DeLeo doesn't do that again."

Hector deftly prepared a syringe, tapping the top. Fluid squirted from the tip. Hector neared, and DeLeo squirmed as best he could but it was no use. Everything went black.

DeLeo woke to blurry white lights. When his eyes adjusted, he was in another cell, this one quite different from the last. It had padded walls like an insane asylum. He tried to move his arms, but they had put him in a straight jacket.

"Let's try this again," Dr. Stone said from the doorway.

DeLeo lifted his head. His thoughts were foggy. "Am I still on TV?" he asked.

"Someone is always watching here. Now, why do you think you are here?"

"This is torture!"

"This is an intervention, Mr. DeLeo. Can you think why?"

"I want to go home."

"I can't allow that until I've seen positive changes in your condition."

"What condition? You did this to me!"

"Tell me about your family, your daughter. If you don't confront your past, you'll never get better."

DeLeo felt like he was reverting to a childish state. "I'm better now, I swear. I've learned my lesson."

"How can I believe you? You've lied in the past to get what you want, so why not now?"

"I want my music. It will help me think clearly."

"I'll think about it." Dr. Stone quickly left, shutting the door behind her.

"I want out of here!" DeLeo pleaded, screaming into the padded walls in vain.

11

DeLeo woke to drool pooling in his arms. The drugs were wearing off. Blurry images moved past his face, but couldn't make out what they were or where he was. He slowly looked down at his arms, realizing he was no longer tied or shackled. His arms rested on the wings of a wheelchair. He tried to move his them but couldn't. They were heavy, numb to the touch. The drugs still had their hold. He could barely move his fingers. Giving up, he dozed off again.

He woke sometime later, still in the wheelchair, but his clothes had been changed. He wore an all-white outfit, like something a hospital patient would wear. Surveying his surroundings, he realized he was in a medical ward with five other drooling vegetables, each with a look of confusion and utter stupidity on their faces as they gazed blindly at the television.

DeLeo tried to wiggle his toes and then his fingers. No use. He knew they had pumped him full of so much shit they could probably pull out a tooth, and he wouldn't feel it. The changing television channel stopped, "I love this show," DeLeo heard a voice say from behind him. DeLeo glacially turned his head to see where the sound came from. It was a big man, with bright eyes, and the head the size of a cantaloupe. He looked familiar, but DeLeo couldn't place him. Was it the drugs or had he really seen this guy somewhere before?

"This is my favorite show," the man said with a child's excitement. The man moved across the room of drooling zombies, gently rolling their wheelchairs out of his way.

"Hey it's you," the man said staring at DeLeo. "From the TV show. I've never met anyone famous before. My name is Tim." The man grabbed DeLeo's limp arm and shook his hand. Tim pointed to the screen.

DeLeo slowly turned his head toward the TV. It was the footage of DeLeo chasing Sadie through the hotel hallway.

"I was in season one," Tim said, with a bright smile that reminded DeLeo of the cartoons he watched as a kid. Cartoons that bordered on lunacy.

DeLeo moved his lips trying to speak, but nothing came out.

Tim moved closer wiping the long stream of spittle oozing from DeLeo's mouth, "Ewww. They got you pumped full of juice, Wes. You can barely speak."

Suddenly DeLeo's memory cleared and he remembered where he recognized Tim from. He was the guy in the Endz Casino & Resort promo video he first saw when he woke up at the poker table. The fat guy stuffing himself full of food. That was him.

"Season one and you're still here?" DeLeo managed to stutter out of his numb mouth.

"Yup," Tim said slapping DeLeo on the back. He

leaned in close. "Shh...he might be listening. Mr. Johnson is smart. He's always one step ahead of us, planning, plotting, conniving. His lackeys everywhere, their eyes and ears always perked. Just when you think you got it figure out he changes the game. These people, the nurses, Dr. Stone, they want to play with our minds, make us crazy. Experiment." Tim pulled back and made a circling motion around his ear with his hand—the international symbol of lunacy, then flashed his cartoonish grin and winked.

Hector entered the room. Tim leaned back and pretended to be a vegetable gazing at the TV, which now was on the scene of DeLeo attacking Sadie in the closet.

Out of the corner of his eye DeLeo watched Hector make his way through the pack of drooling patients dispersing a paper cup full of medicine. He then gave the medicine to Tim, but when Hector turned his back and made his way toward DeLeo, Tim stuck out his tongue revealing two pills still on his tongue.

Hector opened DeLeo mouth and put two pills in and held his nose so he would swallow. DeLeo moved the two tablets to the corner of his mouth so they wouldn't go down his throat and swallowed. DeLeo patiently waited for Hector to leave, before sticking out his tongue revealing the pills to Tim.

When Hector finally left Tim spat the pills into the radiator in the corner of the room. DeLeo did the same thing. He could feel his strength coming back to him. He could now move his upper body.

"Don't trust anyone," Tim said, "They probably have microphones and cameras in the walls."

DeLeo glanced at the corners of the room and saw nothing but he knew that didn't matter. Camera's could be anywhere. "How do I know I can trust you?" DeLeo asked Tim.

"Of course, of course," Tim responded, with an odd, lop-sided grin, "You can't trust me," he said in a high-pitched almost hysterical voice. "You can't trust anyone."

"Who are all these people? These zombies?"

Tim scanned the room, "Former contestants just like you and me."

"How long have they been here?"

"Who knows. They probably don't even know. They take the drugs, numb their minds, like you used to do, and spend the rest of their day watching TV. They're so out of it they don't even know where they are anymore." Tim grabbed DeLeo's arm and rolled up his sleeve. "I see that's something you've experienced before."

DeLeo quickly pulled his arm away and rolled down the sleeve of his gown, covering the track marks on his arm.

"That's all in the past."

"Old habits die hard," Tim said.

"How does a place like this exist?" DeLeo said changing the subject, "This can't be legal."

Tim ran his hand through his thinning hair, "We all signed on the dotted line or were committed by someone else. Unless we were hospitalized before, like an overdose." The inflection in his voice made DeLeo think he was specifically talking about him.

"I know how I got here," DeLeo said defensively. "They drugged me and shipped me out."

"Or that's what they want you to think," Tim grinned. "I told you Mr. Johnson is smart, always one step a head of you. How you got here doesn't matter anymore. After they got you to attack the girl in the closet it changed everything. You're screwed. Just another number." Tim motioned to the other vegetables gazing at the TV. "Just like them."

"There has to be a way out of here."

Tim's playful demeanor disappeared, "There's no way out of here. I've tried. Get used to it. Enjoy the simple things, and don't think too much, or you'll really go crazy. You could always take the pills and watch TV for the rest of your life just like them." Tim's eyes moved to the salivating patients. "I mean, people do it all the time out in the real world. Binging sports, reality TV, or a whole season of some damn show in a day. And most of those people aren't even committed!" Tim burst into laugher and slapped DeLeo on the back like some old friend. "You and me have to stick together."

The next morning DeLeo pretended to take the pills before he was rolled into the interrogation cell. Dr. Stone was waiting along with Hector and three other orderlies.

"I see you've made friends with one of our former contestants," Dr. Stone said with her best poker face.

"You mean prisoners," DeLeo said. His head was now clear. His body was rested.

"Patients," Dr. Stone corrected with an easy smile.

"Has it ever crossed your mind that maybe all of this, the TV show, your games, your poking and prodding, is immoral?"

Dr. Stone nodded her head as if she had thought about this question before. "It's easy to think like that when you don't have all the details, Mr. DeLeo. Your new friend Tim Sherman is a long-standing patient of mine. If you saw his file, you might think a little differently." Dr. Stone adjusted her glasses. "He has serious problems and needs constant supervision. We don't have him in our care for some trivial reason."

"He seemed fine to me."

"Mr. DeLeo, your diagnosis is noted but please leave it to the experts. This meeting is about you not one of our other patients, so how are you feeling?"

"I'm fine. Tip-top, "DeLeo said forcing a smile.

"You do look better," Dr. Stone inspected his eyes with a flashlight, then pointed to a camera in the ceiling. "I do know you stopped taking your medication."

"Don't I have any privacy?"

"I'm afraid not, but I will permit you to stop taking the medication for now. But if I see any signs of aggression, this whole process will start all over again. You understand?"

DeLeo bit his lip and nodded his head.

"Good," Dr. Stone crossed her arms. "I do believe social interaction is a critical part of rehabilitation. Please don't make me regret this." Dr. Stone smiled and motioned for Hector to open the cell door.

"Dr. Stone," DeLeo began, politely using her name for the first time.

"Yes, Wes?" she seemed pleasantly surprised by his civility.

"Can I have my guitar?"

Dr. Stone considered his request, "You've shown some progress, so I will permit it—temporarily. Hector, please see to it Mr. DeLeo has his instrument."

An hour later DeLeo was out of his wheelchair and sitting in the ward lobby with his acoustic guitar. He didn't care if his audience were a bunch of slobbering lunatics. He was relieved to have his guitar in his hands. He felt complete again, like and amputee whose arm or a leg had just been returned to him.

He let his fingers gently strum the strings. He thought of his daughter Delilah and how he taught her first chord a few years back between one of his now endless tour cycles. He imagined his wife sitting next to him and how bitter she must feel for being involved with this show. He wanted to kiss her. Apologize for what she went through and truly make up for all those years he was away on the road going from one dive bar to the other.

The pain melted away like butter every time he strummed the guitar. He started to sing and for the first time since the game show, he felt at peace. When he finished the song, he heard applause. He looked up and saw Tim Sherman standing behind the group of vegetables, clapping with his giant cartoon grin. "Great job, very well done."

"Thanks," DeLeo said.

Tim walked toward DeLeo pushing the patients out of the way until he was in front of DeLeo. Tim crouched down and whispered. "I found a way out?"

"What do you mean?" DeLeo replied.

"Shh, they'll hear you," Tim said softly looking at the orderlies in the far corner of the ward. "I was thinking, and then it all came to me,"

DeLeo leaned in curiously, "What, what came to you?"

"Push the reset button," Tim said.

"Push the reset button? What are you talking about?"

"Start all over again," Tim said matter-of-factly. "This isn't real. None of it is," his voice getting louder and more passionate. "This is just TV. There's no reason to be afraid anymore."

"Tim, relax," Hector said from the other side of the ward room.

Tim ignored him and raised his hands above his head, "Series finale man. It's all over. I found a way out."

Hector and another orderly moved closer to Tim anticipating a breakdown.

"Be quiet," DeLeo said, watching the white coats drawing closer. "They'll take you down and pump you full of juice."

"But I found a way out Wes. It's okay."

"Calm down Tim," Hector warned growing nearer.

DeLeo could tell the white coats were coordinating with each other, preparing to follow protocol for when a patient finally snaps.

"Mr. Sherman," Dr. Stone said entering the room. "Settle down, or we'll have to sedate you and put you back in your room. You don't want to go back into your room, do you?"

"It's okay, it's okay," Tim said like a broken record. "It's okay. It's okay."

"Tim," DeLeo said, "Quit acting crazy. Be quiet."

"Maybe there's nothing wrong with being a little crazy Wes," Tim dug for something in his pocket. DeLeo couldn't tell what it was. "Push the reset button Wes. Push it."

Tim flashed his loony cartoon grin and quickly jerked his hand up to his neck jamming something into his throat. Blood squirted in every direction. Tim continued to stab the object into his neck over and over, all the while maintaining the same comical smirk across his face.

Suddenly, Tim turned pale and dropped to his knees, still jabbing toward his throat. The white coats rushed over to him and tried to get him to stop.

DeLeo watched in disgust as Tim mutilated himself. Blood drenched the room. Tim burped his final breath in a giant pool of red. The other vegetables gazed at the madness like it was no different from some TV show. Their eyes were blank, their faces numb.

Anger consumed DeLeo as he watched Dr. Stone inspect Tim's body. How did they let him do this to himself, DeLeo wondered, shocked and confused.

Chip swiftly entered the room followed by two producers wearing headsets. A look of disbelief registered on his face. "Oh my god!" Chip said, looking at the blood. It was everywhere. He ran to Tim's body and felt his pulse. "He's dead Helen," he said, directing his anger at Dr. Stone. "I thought you said you had this under control!"

"I did. Well, I thought I did," Dr. Stone responded in a panic. Her hands were shaking. She looked to Hector trying to deflect responsibility. "I thought you were watching?"

"Shut up!" Chip screamed at Dr. Stone. "You're responsible. This is a TV show for Christ sakes. Where did he get the knife?"

"I don't know," Dr. Stone pleaded. "One of us must have missed it."

"We got to get rid of the body," Chip said. "We cannot have anyone asking questions."

Dr. Stone looked toward Hector and the other white coats for backup, but they remained stoic and in shock. "Mr. Sherman doesn't have a family," Dr. Stone said quickly. "I mean he's from season one, people don't even watch those episodes anymore. No one will miss him."

"You better take care of this," Chip demanded.

"I will. I will."

DeLeo was in disbelief. It was their fault that Tim was dead and now they were going cover it up. Like he never existed. Push the delete button on his whole life.

"It's all your fault!" DeLeo shouted at Dr. Stone from across the room. "And yours," DeLeo charged Chip holding the guitar like a baseball bat and swung. He slipped on the bloody floor, missing Chip, but smashing the wooden guitar into the face of one of the orderlies. DeLeo attempted to get to his feet but was tackled by Hector. He felt Hector's knee on his back and his arms locked behind him in some impossible to escape hold.

"Get him out of here now!" Chip screamed.

"Sir, I don't have any sedatives on me," Hector gasped holding DeLeo to the floor.

"Who gives a shit," Chip demanded, "Just lock him up.

We'll take care of him later. We have to clean this mess up now."

Hector and the remaining orderlies dragged DeLeo out of the ward and down the hallway toward his cell. The last sound DeLeo heard before he was thrown into the padded chamber was Chip barking orders. "Make sure whatever footage you have is deleted. We can't have any of this getting out."

12

White coats rushed past the portal window in the padded cell. DeLeo couldn't see far enough out of the small hole to tell what they were doing, but he could sense from the muffled voices that Tim Sherman's suicide and cleanup occupied them all.

DeLeo lay on the narrow bed. He wondered what they would do to him next. Would they try and drug him again or would they try to get rid of him and make up some story like did with Tim Sherman?

He would put up a fight, that was certain. Kick, punch, eye-gouge, bite whoever put their hands on him next. He was prepared to sink to their level even if it meant jamming his hand down Hector's throat. They would have to kill him, he thought. He was ready to die if it meant taking one of those savages down with him.

DeLeo listened to the muffled sounds outside growing fainter. They had enough surprises for today, he thought, no way they were going to deal with him tonight. Use this time to rest up, he thought. Prepare to fight tomorrow.

DeLeo nestled comfortably on the bed and closed his eyes.

Suddenly he heard a scratch, like a fingernail or a knife, on the door. He opened his eyes and stared at the door. A piece of paper slid underneath.

DeLeo sat up curiously and watched as the paper came to a floating stop in front of his hospital-issued flip flops. He picked it up. It was a note. He turned it over. In all capital letters, it read: UNDER THE MATTRESS.

DeLeo paused for a moment, thinking about what it could mean. He decided to do what the note seemed to be telling him. He picked up the mattress with one hand and looked underneath. A gas mask was placed in the corner of the bed frame. He stared at it, carefully and suspiciously inspecting every part.

Suddenly, an explosion erupted in the ward outside the cell. DeLeo flinched. He looked through the porthole. There was smoke that, seconds later, began to seep through the small cracks in the door.

DeLeo put on the mask hoping it was sealed correctly. A quick rapid succession of gunfire followed from outside. Alarmed and confused, he backed away from the door against the soft padded walls.

There was a thud against the door, blood smeared the small oval window. DeLeo's eyes widened. What was happening?

Another note slid under the door. He picked it up, squinting through the bug-eye lens of the gas mask.

STAND BACK! the note read.

"Stand back?" DeLeo repeated aloud, confused. Then he realized. "Stand back!" He quickly dove to the other side of the room, taking cover behind the bed.

The cell door exploded. The door flew across the room, landing next to DeLeo. The small space quickly flooded with smoke. Through the thick smoke, DeLeo could make out the shape of what looked like a soldier dressed in dark green military fatigues holding a machine gun and wearing a gas mask.

The gun exploded in rapid-fire down the hallway, the muzzle flare like a giant fireball flashing through the cloud of smoke.

DeLeo's head was ringing as the solider stopped firing and approached him, extending his hand. DeLeo hesitated for a moment, trying to read the soldiers eyes through the mask, but he couldn't see anything. He blindly grabbed for the soldier's hand.

Before DeLeo knew it, he was following the soldier down the narrow, smoked-filled halls of the ward. The soldier signaled for DeLeo to hit the ground. Machine gun fire erupted from the other side of the room, ripping apart the plaster wall behind him. The soldier quickly returned fire, ending the threat.

The soldier nudged the limp body of one of the blue uniformed security forces as they passed to confirm that the threat was, indeed, neutralized.

"What the hell is going on?" DeLeo questioned the soldier, who ignored him and pulled him along to keep them moving.

Without warning, a muzzle flash ripped from the end of the soldier's machine gun as they entered the main wardroom. Shapes and shadows of heavily armed security forces wearing blue military fatigues burst into the room.

Gunfire roared from all directions. The soldier flipped over the couch and pulled DeLeo to the ground. The tile floor was still a faint red, stained with Tim Sherman's blood.

The soldier returned fire at the security forces across the room then quickly ducked behind the couch, grabbing a magazine, reloading, then unhooked a grenade tossing it across the room.

Moments later a large flash lit the cloud of smoke.

The soldier motioned for DeLeo to remain there then disappeared into the mist. DeLeo stayed low, lifting his eyes just above the couch. Muffled flashes in the smoke and the crack of gunfire was all DeLeo could see and hear.

Hurry up, he pleaded silently. He didn't want to be left here alone.

Something strong grabbed him from behind, his feet dragging across the tile floor as he tried to get traction and figure out what was going on.

It was Hector. He pulled DeLeo into a nearby room and threw him on top of a hospital bed as three more white coats pinned him down, ripped off his mask, and began to strap his arms and legs to the bed.

"You're not going anywhere," Dr. Stone announced, emerging from a dark corner of the room. She held a syringe in one hand and a silver pistol in the other.

"Let me out!" DeLeo screamed, trying his best to fight out of the straps.

"You have two choices," Dr. Stone said, stonefaced, looking first at the syringe, then at the pistol.

Suddenly the door burst open. Muzzle fire flashed through the room, followed by screams. DeLeo felt the warm spray of fresh blood across his face and heard the sound of what could only be bodies dropping to the floor.

He looked down. Dr. Stone, Hector, and the other white coats were all lifeless on the floor, covered in blood.

The soldier approached DeLeo, pulling out a massive survival knife and cutting the straps, freeing DeLeo. Wes slowly got off the hospital bed and inspected the bedlam around him.

"We have you surrounded!" one of the security force

team leaders yelled from outside the room.

"What do we do?" DeLeo whispered, terrified, putting his gas mask back on. They were trapped. That door was their only way out.

The soldier took a rope from his belt and tied it around one of the massive medical machines in the room. He then clipped DeLeo to him.

"What are you doing?" DeLeo asked

The soldier pointed in the opposite direction of the hall-way from where the security force were waiting.

"Are you serious?" DeLeo countered. "That's a dead end!"

"We'll give you to the count of five," the same voice yelled from across the ward. DeLeo looked at the soldier, who was busy unhooking grenades from his belt. DeLeo's eyes widened. The soldier nodded his head, flipped off the ends of each projectile and tossed them out the door into the smoke-filled ward.

After the explosion, the soldier grabbed DeLeo and ran out the door, both of them breathing heavily through the filters of their masks as they moved down the corridor to-ward the window at the dead end. Staring straight ahead, the soldier leveled his machine gun, shot the glass, and without hesitation, the two of them jumped through.

DeLeo and the soldier free-fell from the window. Bricks and windows from the outside of the building moved past. Suddenly, the rope grabbed. DeLeo's body snapped back and everything stopped.

DeLeo and the soldier dangled off the side of the build-ing. It was dark; so dark that he could barely see the yellow light streaming out of the shattered window above. Below, the ground was nowhere in sight.

The soldier clicked something on his belt, and the two of them descended through the clouds.

"Faster!" DeLeo implored. "They could cut the rope any minute!"

The soldier remained steady as the two of them dropped down the side of the building. A colorful blur slowly came into focus as they neared the ground. DeLeo noticed, with as sinking feeling overcoming him, that the light came from the entrance to the casino. The bright Endz Casino & Resort sign illuminated the ground below. They were inside the set of the post-apocalyptic city.

The solider unhooked DeLeo from the rope when they touched the ground. Wes walked toward the casino window, cupped his hands, and looked inside. It was dark and empty but DeLeo could see the outlines of slot machines and poker tables next to studio cameras.

"Where is everyone?" DeLeo asked.

The soldier ignored DeLeo. He was busy prying open a utility hole cover in the street. When he was finished, the soldier snapped his fingers and pointed to the hole.

"In there?" DeLeo asked, more confused than ever.

Soldier nodded and DeLeo entered the hole.

The sewer was dark and wet and even more ominous as the soldier closed the manhole behind them. DeLeo's feet were cold; the ward issued flip-flops didn't protect against much in the ankle deep water.

"So what do we do now, Batman?" DeLeo asked, half joking.

As usual, the soldier said nothing, which was really beginning to annoy DeLeo, but he followed him none-the-less.

The flashlight on the end of the soldier's machine gun cut through the dark, bobbing up and down as they walked through the tunnel. They passed leaking pipes, corroded from years of neglect. Massive rats scurried along the ledge just above the water line.

DeLeo was relieved to be free of Dr. Stone and the white coats, but he had never imagined an escape like this. The sewer felt like a tomb. Deteriorating brick mixed with rusted reinforced steel seemed to be the only thing providing any support from the whole apocalyptic city-set collapsing down on them from above.

The water was up to their shins now and getting deeper. A few steps later, it was at waist level. DeLeo considered asking the soldier where they were going but he knew it wouldn't help. He slipped on something disgusting under his flip flops, grabbed for a slimy pipe, but caught himself before he went down.

They rounded a corner where DeLeo saw a red bulb in the distance and a doorway underneath. It looked like the end of the tunnel. Could it be? DeLeo breathed a sigh of relief when the water returned to knee level and then to ankle level. By the time they reached the red light they were back on dry ground. DeLeo was cold and soaking wet, but he felt as though maybe, just maybe, the worst part was over.

They passed through the doorway and continued. DeLeo was confused and lost in this maze of underground tunnels. He would never be able to find his way back, not that he planned to return.

They reached a dead end and the soldier rotated a rusted hand crank on the wall, revealing a high-tech glowing green keypad.

The soldier typed a code in the keypad and the wall moved, revealing a secret passageway. The sound of voices and commotion was close. There were people just up ahead.

The soldier unbuckled his mask and pulled if off, shaking his head. A clump of red hair tumbled out of the mask. De-Leo couldn't believe what he saw. Ethel, or whatever her

real name was, was the soldier. The religious fundamentalist. The actor. She stood right in front of him holding a
machine gun and smiling. Her skin was like porcelain, her
hair blood red. She had been the one who rescued him.

"Surprised?" Ethel grinned.

"Kind of," DeLeo managed to spit out, utterly shocked.

"Come on Wes. You're safe now. There are some people
I want you to meet. I'll explain everything once we're inside."

DeLeo forced the old image of Ethel out of his mind, in-
trigued by this new version and somewhat stunned by her
natural beauty. He followed her inside toward the voices.

13

The secret tunnel opened up into a vast, two-level underground cave. It looked like a command center, a bunker, for some massive operation. Despite his best efforts, DeLeo couldn't process what he was witnessing.

On the bottom level, there had to be at least twenty or thirty soldiers, some preparing military-style weapons and studying maps, others sparring in preparation for some future combat operation. On the top level, the blue glow of state-of-the-art computers lit the faces of young men and women staring intently at screens.

Ethel pointed at one of the large LCD monitors hanging on the wall in front of them. The screen consisted of a bunch of small squares showing video footage from multiple locations, many of which DeLeo immediately recognized. There was footage of the empty casino studio as well as from the post-apocalyptic city-set, the sewer tunnels, the courtyard ballroom, and the hospital ward room.

"We hacked into their video feed. We've been monitoring you since you arrived in the ward," Ethel said. "We knew we had to act when we saw Tim Sherman lose himself to madness. We couldn't let that happen to you too."

"Wait," DeLeo said stopping in the middle of the bunker. "First I thought you were a zealot, then you were an actor, now you're...what?"

"She's a freedom fighter," a gruff, bearded man answered, walking toward them. "A member of the resistance like the rest of us." The man was dressed in similar green military fatigues and wore a beret.

"That's right," Ethel said. "The acting gig was a cover. My way in. I'm sorry I couldn't have been honest with you from the start. I had to be careful. If they ever found out who I really was the whole operation would have been in jeopardy."

"Operation? What the hell is this, and who are you, really?"

"We are the MLA," Ethel said.

"What the hell is the MLA?"

"Media Liberation Army. I'm Raul Cortez," the bearded man continued. "We are dedicated to the overthrow of media conglomerates: CNN, Fox News, MSNBC, New York Times, Facebook, Google, you get the idea. The list goes on."

"Are you serious?" DeLeo with a hint of sarcasm.

Ethel nodded her head.

"I don't get it. Who are you fighting for?'

Cortez stroked his jet-black beard. "We're for the people. They are being poisoned by what is being fed to them online, through the mainstream media, whether print or on TV. Once the left and right get to the elite levels of government, universities, media, they all spout the same dogma. Control and obedience. The tone of the various media groups may be different, or the way they manipulate their constituencies, but it's all the same in the end. That's why we need a complete revolution."

DeLeo shook his head. What this wanna-be Che Guevara was spouting, was crazy "Media Liberation Army?" He responded in disbelief, "Who came up with that name? It's ridiculous."

"Is it?" Cortez adjusted his beret. "If it wasn't for us they would have pumped you so full of drugs you might as well be dead."

DeLeo looked toward Ethel, "Is this real or is this just another part of this stupid show?"

"Did those bullets fired at our heads seem real?" Ethel responded "What about the blood? What about Tim Sherman?"

There was no doubt what he just witnessed seemed real. "It did," DeLeo conceded. "It's just a lot to wrap my head around at the moment."

"I understand," Cortez said. "It was tough for all of us once we realized the truth."

Wes noticed Ethel's eyes begin to water. "I've had a personal vendetta to go after Chip Johnson since my brother disappeared in their custody ten years ago." Her mouth quivered, but her tears never fell. "Believe me this is serious. They used him because they thought he didn't have any family left, but they were wrong." Ethel loaded a fresh magazine into her gun, then motioned toward the soldiers training. "We need you, Wes. You're the only one who can help us bring them down."

"How did you find me?" DeLeo asked, still skeptical.

Cortez showed DeLeo a tablet of all the video feeds."Our eyes are everywhere." He enlarged one of the camera feeds and live footage of the ward appeared. Chip Johnson stepped over the dead security force bodies as he surveyed the chaos and death in the ward.

Cortez activated the sound. "This was a bloodbath,"

Chip said to one of the surviving members of the security force next to him. "He must have had help and I have a pretty good idea who is behind this."

The footage changed camera angles. Chip Johnson peered out the shattered building window where DeLeo and Ethel had jumped. He kicked some of the remaining glass and watched it fall into the darkness. Sadie entered the frame and joined Chip at his side.

"She a friend of yours too?" DeLeo asked Ethel and Cortez, pointing to Sadie.

"God no," Ethel said. "Just an actor like the others. However, now that she is with Chip Johnson it seems like she is getting more involved with the whole operation."

DeLeo watched the massive screen showing Chip and Sadie standing at the edge of the window like the finale to a love story and muttered,"If I was there right now, I would push her out the window."

Ethel chucked. "Stick with us, and you just might get your chance."

When they finished watching the footage of Sadie and Chip surveying the ruins of the ward, DeLeo followed Ethel through the underground command center. It was like the structure had been built in right from the ground. They passed old industrial pipes and steel until they reached a door that looked like it belonged on a submarine.

"You can get cleaned up in here," Ethel opened the door. The chamber looked like an old boiler room transformed into a living space. "The water isn't warm," she added, "but it's clean. There are fresh clothes on the bed."

DeLeo felt grateful for what she had done. Two hours ago he had watched Tim Sherman jam a shank into his own neck and thought they were going to lock him away forever or worse, kill him. Now he was free.

"Ethel," DeLeo said. "I appreciate everything you've

done for me."

She smiled. "My real name is Liz. Rest up. We need you strong and ready. After the mess I made getting you out, there's no doubt they'll try and find us. And when they do, they'll hit us with everything they got."

DeLeo sat on the corner of the bed. "It's hard to wrap my head around all this. The show, the hospital ward, the MLA. My mind is spinning."

"Well, you've been through a lot," Ethel said, comforting DeLeo. "I can understand how this can be confusing. I mean the last time you saw me I wasn't too nice," she smiled. He face now warm and trusting, like an old friend.

DeLeo laughed. "That's an understatement."

"It was hard watching you go through all that. I wanted to help you from the beginning, but I couldn't risk it. At least not then." DeLeo saw Ethel glance down at the track marks on his arms. "No matter what happens in life there's always so much left unfinished. Do you know what I mean Wes?"

"I do," DeLeo said, tears coming to his eyes. "I spent all my time running from the things that were the most important to me. The things that really mattered – my family. My wife and daughter. Now all that's gone."

"It isn't over yet," Ethel smiled. "We're going to get you out of here. Now get some rest."

Ethel left the room. DeLeo showered and crawled into bed. The mattress was soft and comforting. He felt like he could sleep for days. He shut his eyes and drifted off.

14

Suddenly, he woken by a thundering explosion. He didn't know how long he was asleep, and hour maybe two. Groggy and unaware of his surroundings, he jumped out of bed.

Cortez and Ethel ran in, shouting warnings to hurry. DeLeo quickly put on the clothes and military grade boots Ethel had given him and, at her signal, cautiously cracked open the door.

Smoke and fire filled the bunker. It was a war zone. Without warning, another explosion ripped through the command center spraying brick and debris everywhere.

"They're inside! They found us!" DeLeo heard someone yell through the dust and smoke filling the room. The sound of gunfire tore through the cave.

Cortez and Ethel emerged from the cloud of smoke and debris. "How did they get in?" Cortez yelled.

"Move!" Ethel yelled, pushing Cortez out of the way. She raised her machine gun and fired at the heavily armed security force spilling into the large hole that had been blasted into the wall.

White muzzle flash exploded from the tip of her weapon, cutting the blue uniforms down.

"We have to get upstairs. It's our only chance!" Cortez yelled.

Keeping his head down, DeLeo followed Ethel and Cortez to the second level of the bunker, pausing and ducking for cover as they laid down machine fire. He watched as soldiers on both sides were mutilated from the high-powered weapons. No one was safe. The security force seemed better armed and more prepared this time than they had been before. They carried riot shields, stronger body armor and larger weapons.

When DeLeo, Cortez, and Ethel made it to the top level of the bunker, DeLeo dove under one of the computer consoles for cover. More explosions and gunfire filled the underground cavern, followed by screams and the ever-present sound of grown men wailing in agony.

Every few moments DeLeo would look through a crack in the console to see Ethel or Cortez spraying machine gun fire over the railing.

Blue uniforms fell to the ground, snapping like guitar strings, peppered with bullets. Screams of atrocious pain and sprays of blood covered the bunker. There was no way this was staged. What DeLeo was witnessing was the closest thing to all-out war he could possibly imagine. Bullets hitting the steel desk next to him left indents. The sound from the explosion still rang in his ears.

"Get him out of here!" Cortez yelled to Ethel. "The extraction team will be here in twenty minutes."

Ethel's machine gun roared, picking off different security forces below. She stopped to reload, looked at her watch, and ran over to DeLeo.

Before either of them could speak, a bullet hit Cortez right between the eyes. His head snapped back, chunks of flesh sprayed against the wall, and he collapsed to the ground. DeLeo was speechless.

It was a massacre. The resistance had been caught off guard. Bodies were scattered everywhere. Other than Ethel and DeLeo, it seemed that no one was left alive. Ethel grabbed DeLeo by the shirt. "We're out of time. We have to go now."

DeLeo could hear what he assumed were the blue uniformed security forces ascending the stairs to the second level of the bunker.

"This way," Ethel pulled DeLeo to the back, where a catwalk led down a narrow corridor.

"It's a dead end!" DeLeo yelled, seeing no way out.

"Not for you it isn't," Ethel yelled, firing at the first soldiers up the stairs.

The further down the corridor they went, DeLeo and Ethel took cover from the fire in small nooks. DeLeo looked around for any way out but saw nothing. The only way out was back the way they came.

Ethel kicked out a nearby grate in the wall revealing a small two by two opening. "Get in!" she yelled.

DeLeo didn't hesitate, didn't stop to consider his alternative. He scurried into the small hole feet first while Ethel laid down, covering fire.

"This is an old sewer system," she explained quietly, reloading a magazine. "Once you get to the other side, take the tunnel down until you see a ladder. It will take you to the surface level." She lay down more gunfire.

"Then what?" DeLeo yelled.

"The extraction team. They'll meet you there." Ethel took her watch off and handed it to DeLeo. "There is a tracker in here. You have fifteen minutes. Be there. If you're not, they'll leave you. It's too dangerous here now. Promise me you'll be there?"

DeLeo took the watch and strapped it to his wrist. "I'll be there. But what about you?"

Ethel grinned. "I'm not going anywhere. Remember, I'm the one with the big gun." She effortlessly lay down a steady stream of gunfire and quickly reloaded. "Go on," she shouted. "I'll be right behind you."

DeLeo backed into the ventilation shaft but before he could get far, Ethel was hit by three shots, exploding her chest on impact. She fell to the ground, still continuing to fire.

"Get out of here," she gasped, spitting up blood and motioning down the shaft. Maroon liquid pooled around her. Her eyes began to fade. "You have to survive. This was all for you." Ethel removed two grenades from her belt. "I'm not going without taking at least a few of those bastards with me. Go now."

Shocked and saddened by what had just happened, DeLeo faltered for a second. "Thank you," he said, choking up and then, regaining his composure, he quickly crawled through the ventilation shaft.

The shaft was tight and greasy but he kept moving. The echo of distant gunfire filled the small space. He suddenly spilled out in the opening covered in dirt and filth.

Suddenly, Ethel's grenades detonated and an explosion lit the small tube. A massive flame shot out of the ventilation shaft just above DeLeo's head as he instinctively dove to the ground for cover. The smell of burnt hair and flesh filled the small area. DeLeo checked the watch: 5 minutes. He could hear the voices of the security forces through the tunnel. Ethel hadn't been able to kill them all.

DeLeo ran down the tunnel until he came to the ladder Ethel told him about. Hand over hand he made it up the cold, wet rungs as fast as he could, praying the extraction team wouldn't leave him behind. His arms burned. His ears rung. The muffled noise of the security force was close behind.

15

Blinking, DeLeo exited the utility hole. White light flooded his eyes. It was daytime for sure, but the fog was so thick he could barely see ten feet in front of him. He stood on what felt like pavement and what seemed to be an empty parking lot. There was no one there. No extraction team waiting.

He checked the watch: 2 minutes remained.

Cold sweat ran down his face at the thought of being left behind. He had to see his family again. Amber, Delilah, they were the only things that mattered. He moved into the fog away from the utility hole to put some distance between him and whoever was on his tail. He prayed the tracker on the watch worked and that the extraction team would be able to find him.

The crackle of radio chatter burst through the silence, followed by boots on pavement. The security forces were there. It had to be them, somewhere in the fog. DeLeo didn't know where for sure, but he knew they had to be close.

Suddenly the rotating swoosh of helicopter blades came from above, breaking DeLeo's focus. Ethel's watch began to glow a neon blue. The extraction team, DeLeo thought. They were here. Though he couldn't see them, the helicopter had to be the team.

He ran toward the sound of the helicopter blades. He still couldn't see anything through the white mist and used his ears to guide him. The closer he got to the swoosh of the helicopter blades, the bluer his watch became. Suddenly, he slammed full-speed into a chain linked railing.

The fog began to thin out and it was only then he noticed he was standing at the edge of a massive cliff that descended into what seemed like infinity. The pavement under his feet seemed to just end. If it weren't for the chain railing, he would have toppled over, careened into the abyss.

The sound of the helicopter slowly faded into the distance and the blue glow of his watch and hope for freedom dimmed with it.

Standing on the edge of the cliff, DeLeo turned to face an abundance of military boots and radio chatter coming toward him. They were so close. His heart began to pound slower and what felt like deeper. It became harder to breathe and he felt as though he was going to pass out. There was no redemption, no extraction team, just the sound of boots on pavement getting closer by the second. This was the end.

Then, just as suddenly as it started, everything stopped. The boots, the radio, the bouncing utility belts. All of it was gone.

Silence.

A cold gust of wind blew along the edge of the cliff, twisting and twirling the fog that eventually lifted to reveal Chip Johnson standing no more than ten feet away.

"Long way down, huh?" Chip mused, lifting an eyebrow.

DeLeo was shocked. He couldn't believe what he was seeing once again.

"Is this real??" DeLeo asked. "Are those people really dead back there or are you still messing with me? Where are the cameras?" DeLeo shouted, his agony piercing the otherwise silent cliff.

"Interesting take on things Wes, but I'm going to have to ask you to come with me."

"I can't go back. I can't. Never."

"We can talk about that later."

The thought of crazy Tim Sherman passed through DeLeo's mind. "Just push the reset button," he remembered Tim saying to him just before he jammed that shank into his neck. "It's the only way out."

DeLeo looked over the edge. There was no way someone would survive a jump from this height. He thought of his wife and daughter, then he thought about being locked in that padded cell for god knows how many years. There's no way they would let him leave. Not this time. They'd pump him full of so much shit, like all those other vegetables, he would never be able to form a coherent thought again.

"What do you mean, later? What's next?" DeLeo pressed, unmoving.

"We'll figure that out later."

"I'm not going back. You'll lock me up for good this time." DeLeo threw his leg over the railing and put his foot down on the six-inch lip. He finally understood what Tim Sherman had done, and why. There was no way out. Once people think you're crazy—that's it. There's no coming back from that.

"What are you doing Wes?" Chip said with what seemed to be newfound compassion. "Don't do it. We can help you."

Tears flowed from Wes's eyes. "You've ruined my life. You took my family away from me. You've taken everything from me. I'm already dead so what does it really matter anymore? This is all your fault."

DeLeo closed his eyes, leaned back, and let himself fall off the edge. He was at peace as the cool air passed through his hair until everything went black.

DeLeo woke to the sound of slot machines ringing in his ears. He was in Endz Casino. Again. Dressed in the same clothes as when he first woke up, before all this craziness began: gray cardigan, black jeans. He rubbed his face and looked around the room. Everything was identical.

Was this still the TV show?

The TV monitor turned on, playing the same Endz Resort & Casino infomercial starring Tim Sherman as the fat, middle-age glutton lounging poolside and stuffing his face with bacon.

"What the hell?" DeLeo mumbled.

"Still hurts, doesn't it?" a familiar voice said.

DeLeo quickly turned around. Chip Johnson stood at the poker table shuffling a deck of cards.

"What the hell is this?"

"I think you already know," Chip replied.

"Where are the cameras, the audience? Where is everyone?"

Chip shrugged.

"Fuck you!" DeLeo screamed. He looked around for a brief second, turned, and ran out of the casino.

The air was the same as he remembered, stale with a hint of sulfur. Light gray fog blanket the dark city. Deja-vu.

"Hello?" DeLeo yelled into the dark.

Silence.

"Your TV show sucks!" he bellowed, once again to silence.

DeLeo thought about going back inside and pounding the hell out of Chip, but the familiar sound of feet dragging broke his concentration. "Oh this game again," he said into the encroaching mist. "I'm going to mess you up buddy. If you come close to me, I will put my fist down your throat. I don't care if you're part of the Screen Actors Guild or some other bullshit union."

DeLeo felt a tug on his pant leg. He looked down. It was Sadie.

"Shh, they'll hear you," Sadie said.

"Sadie?" DeLeo said laughing. "Of course, you'd be here. Let me tell you I'm in a very fragile state right now. So back off or someone's going to get hurt."

"How do you know my name?" Sadie whispered.

DeLeo grabbed her arm and pulled her to her feet.

"Let go of me," Sadie said trying her best to maintain a whisper.

"You know, it has crossed my mind what I would do to you if I ever got the chance to see you again."

"Let go of me! I've never seen you before in my life."

Sadie pulled her arm away from DeLeo and disappeared into the fog. He didn't bother to chase her. He was tired of running.

A figure came into view. Arms extended. Swinging like a pendulum. Same as before.

"Nice suit buddy," DeLeo said. "I'm not going to be nice this time. I'm feeling, well, incredibly violent right now."

The figure walked toward him. DeLeo squeezed his fists as hard as he could. He wanted to bury them as deep as possible into whoever touched him. He looked forward to it. He wanted to hurt whatever piece of shit was wearing that stupid costume, with its cheesy reptilian skin and stupid rubber mask.

"I hope you have insurance. I'm going to rip that thing off your head and punch you in the teeth," DeLeo laughed. "You messed with the wrong guy, pal."

The person came at DeLeo and he swung as hard as he could. His fist connected hard against the slimy surface of the suit. DeLeo grabbed at the head and tried to rip off his mask. It didn't move. Confused, he tried again. His hands slipped.

DeLeo felt a jab and then a sharp pain in his stomach. Before he knew it, he was on the ground gasping for air. The figure stood over him. DeLeo looked around and saw blood. It was everywhere. His intestines seemed to have spilled out on to the pavement.

DeLeo coughed up blood. He felt nauseous.

A high-pitched, agonizing screamed roared from the mouth of the thing that stood over him. DeLeo watched as it raised its razor-like claws, and then everything went black.

◆◆◆

DeLeo woke at the poker table in a cold sweat frantically grabbing at his stomach. He looked down. Everything was fine. No blood, no wound. Back to normal.

The TV turned on, showing the infomercial with Tim Sherman, same as before. Chip Johnson appeared in front of him like he had done every other time.

"This isn't happening, it can't be," DeLeo pleaded. A new sense of dread overcame him at the thought of where he might actually be.

"Oh, but it is," Chip Johnson replied.

"What's your real name?" DeLeo asked

"I go by many names. Chip seems appropriate for now. Very theatrical—daytime TV."

DeLeo ran around the casino and looked behind every door. Bricks—everywhere. "Where is everyone? Where are the cameras? Where's the crew?"

DeLeo didn't wait for Chip to answer. He burst through the revolving door into the dark. Once outside he ran down the red carpet. The fog thickened just like it had done before.

"Hello?" he whispered, hoping in vain for a different result.

After a few moments, he felt a tug at his pants. It was Sadie. Same as before. "Quiet," she whispered.

She offered her help like she had done the first time, only this time DeLeo accepted, pretending he had never met her before. Like clockwork, a groan from one of the creatures came from the fog.

DeLeo waited for Sadie's signal and then the two of them were running through the fog, just as they had done the very first time, the heavy breathing and precise steps of the beasts right behind them.

When they entered the old bank DeLeo quickly stuck out his foot, tripping Sadie. She fell to the ground, crying out in surprise and fear. DeLeo kept running, not once looking back. He heard the creatures crash through the glass and attack Sadie as she tried to get up.

By the time DeLeo heard Sadie's scream, he was already at the vault. He picked up the wrench and banged on the door.

The door opened and DeLeo swung the wrench as hard as he could cracking John in the face. John fell to the ground, his face bloodied, his nose probably broken. DeLeo closed the door to the vault and quickly unclipped John's gun from his belt.

"Don't move," DeLeo yelled, backing himself into the corner so no one could attack him from behind. He pointed the pistol at Ethel, remembering their time together in the bunker. How she had rescued him. Saved his life. The nice things she had said to him. Was that real? he thought. Nothing was real. It wasn't even a dream.

"Don't you remember me?" DeLeo asked her.

Ethel shook her head. She was scared. Terrified. Her eyes teared.

"How can you not remember me?" DeLeo yelled. "None of you?"

"Who are you, pal?" John asked, slowly standing up and using a towel to stop the blood that was now pouring down his face.

"What do you know about this place?" DeLeo asked frantically. "I mean beyond those things. What's out there?"

"Don't tell him anything," John said. "He's all strung out. If you're looking for a fix pal, you won't find it here."

DeLeo pointed the pistol at Tucker and screamed. "Tell me!"

Suddenly, John dropped to the ground, reached for his ankle, and pulled out a small revolver. Two loud cracks followed by quick, bright flashes lit the vault.

DeLeo felt his chest explode then everything went black.

DeLeo woke at the poker table, same as before. His ears were still ringing from the gunshots. He took a deep breath and checked his chest. Everything was fine.

The TV monitor began to play but this time it wasn't the same hotel infomercial. It was something different, footage of the inside of a hospital. Someone was lying in bed, unconscious, hooked up to tubes and monitors. Two people, with their backs toward the camera were also in the room. The heart rate monitor next to the bed slowly pulsed up and down.

"Mrs. DeLeo," a doctor said gently, walking into the room. "Perhaps I can talk to you in private for a moment, without your daughter present."

"She'll have to learn about her father soon enough," Amber said in a fatigued voice, now visible to DeLeo watching from the poker table.

"Your husband," the doctor took a deep breath, "has done significant damage to his body over the years. He's in a coma. With this last overdose, his body couldn't take it anymore. I can't say that we expect him to recover."

Amber wiped the tears from her face and kissed Delilah who stood next to her, shaking.

For the first time, DeLeo saw that it was himself lying in the bed hooked up to the heart monitor, tubes coming out of his mouth and an IV injected next to the track marks on his arm.

DeLeo watched as the heart monitor began to skip beats and finally flat lined. Amber kissed him on the forehead.

The monitor went black.

"You can die a million times here," Chip said from behind him. "But out there, you only get one."

It finally sunk in where DeLeo was and the consequences of his actions that had brought him here.

"Who are those people out there?" DeLeo asked, pointing towards the front of the casino where the whole cast of creatures stood: Sadie, John, Billy, Ethel, Tucker—all of them, watching. Their eyes now distant and sunken in. Gone were the resemblances to anything living.

"You're all here for different reasons," Chip said.

"Why didn't any of them in the recognize me?"

"Everyone is on their own journey. Denial is not easy to overcome. People reach an understanding of what's happening at their own pace." Chip put the deck of cards on the table. "You don't look good Wes. A little dark under the eye maybe? Addiction is a terrible disease."

Overcome with regret and despair, DeLeo said. "I wasted my life, my talents. I was selfish, and I lost my family for it."

"And they lost you," Chip added.

DeLeo wiped his tears. "So now what?"

"Are you ready to play again?"

"Again? Where's the crowd, the cameras, the show?"

Chip smiled. "We don't need that this time."

"No," DeLeo said. "I don't think I can do it."

Chip smiled, "The funny thing is Wes, you don't get to decide."

Suddenly Amber and Delilah entered through the revolving door.

"Daddy!" Delilah exclaimed, running toward DeLeo. "I've missed you."

DeLeo dropped to his knees and scooped up the young girl. He kissed her and said, "I love you. I've missed you so much."

DeLeo felt Amber's arms around him. "I'm so happy to see you," she whispered into his ear.

DeLeo kissed her and smiled. He was so happy to see them again, to feel them in his arms.

"Wait," DeLeo said, pulling away. His mouth ran dry, his heart began to pump harder at the thought of what came next. DeLeo looked toward Chip, his eyes distant, his face straight and stern, showing no emotion, like it had when they first met.

"Is this real or is this another game?" DeLeo asked.

Chip shrugged, then grinned. "You better enjoy it while it lasts." The Dealer picked up the deck of cards off the green felt poker table and dealt.

♠♠♠

THE END

ABOUT THE AUTHOR

Ben is from Massachusetts. In addition to writing he is also a musician and his music can be found on iTunes. You can contact him at @BLarracey on Twitter or visit BenScreenplays.com for more information.

Made in the USA
Middletown, DE
18 November 2018